Crunch

THE RILEY BROTHERS BOOK 4

E. DAVIES

Publisher's Note: This is a work of fiction. Names, characters, places, and incidents are a product of the author's imagination. Locales and public names are sometimes used for atmospheric purposes. Any resemblance to actual people, living or dead, or to businesses, companies, events, institutions, or locales is completely coincidental.

Crunch / E. Davies. – 2nd ed.
ISBN: 978-1-912245-03-1

CHAPTER

One

FLOYD

"Any interesting clients this week?"

Floyd grinned as he leaned back, trying to keep his head straight. "Well, there was one who wants a snake tattoo fixed up. It looked really shitty – I think a buddy of his did it originally. So we've been going over how to fix it, and I think I can cover most of the shittiness up."

"Oh, good." His hairdresser, Christian, teased tufts of hair away to clip one at a time, working his way rapidly around the crown of his head. As he worked, his forearms flexed, a muscle on his inner arm easily visible in the mirror. There were birds tattooed across it – birds Floyd had worked on last year. They weren't fading, either. Good. Christian was taking proper care of them.

"Mm. Other than that, not a lot," Floyd shrugged. "Business has been a little slow for me lately, but Chase's style is really in vogue right now. He's getting a lot of work."

"Mmm. That must be tricky," Christian murmured. "We see cuts go into and out of style all the time, but it's easy to learn them. Well, some are a real bitch to do, and some mesh with our style better... but it's not the same as an art style, I don't think."

"Yeah." Floyd resisted the urge to nod. "Though we do learn other styles. I can do a lot, I just do *best* with my own style."

"That's not too dissimilar. Every hairdresser has his own preferences."

"D'you like doing my cut?" Floyd winked in the mirror, making brief eye contact.

Christian grinned, then nodded. "It's not far off my boyfriend's." He returned his attention to the back of Floyd's head as Floyd winced.

Of course he had a boyfriend already. "Weren't you single last time I came in?" *It was kind of the reason I came back to him... well, I did need a new cut, but still.*

"Yeah, we met last week," Christian smiled. "We were talking online for a while and then we just met and clicked... He's a student in the art school here." He glowed in that annoying little way of new lovers, but Floyd couldn't resent him.

"That's sweet," Floyd answered. "God, I think everyone but me is paired off."

"Oh, not at *all*, darling," Christian grinned. "I hear everything in the chair, believe me. There's a lot of guys out there... looking for their soulmate."

"You're a love therapist, too?"

"You know it," Christian laughed. "Do you want it styled as usual?"

"Yes, please."

"I'll keep an eye out for someone for you, if you'd like," Christian winked as he added a bit of gel and hairspray, then showed him the back with a mirror like usual. Then, they stood up.

Floyd laughed. "Thanks." He dug a bill out of his pocket and handed it over. As usual, he tipped the change even though it was a cheap haircut. He liked the job Christian did, and he came back every month to have it touched up. "Don't worry about it. See you soon. Oh, can I make an appointment for around the first of June?"

"Of course. Big date?" Christian teased. "Ooh, let me guess, a wedding?"

"Not yet, but..." Floyd trailed off. The rate the Rileys were going... "No, a high school reunion."

"Exciting!" Christian typed into the computer. "The first works for me. Morning or afternoon?"

"Morning, please." He took the appointment card when Christian handed it over, then grinned. "Thanks. See you!"

As Floyd strolled out of the shop, his mind wandered. This reunion was going to be miserable without a boyfriend... or at the very least, a date. He could probably rope someone into going, but he was ten years out of high school. Even Thomas was something like a decade younger, yet *he* had a boyfriend.

He knew he shouldn't be worrying about that compared to everything else, but it still grated on his nerves. Maybe he ought to get serious about getting a date... or more. He only had a little more than a month before the reunion, after all.

"And it wouldn't be bad," he murmured as he started up the car.

Well, hopefully.

CHAPTER
Two

GREYSON

"How's the day looking so far?" Greyson sat on the YMCA desk, his knees apart and hands braced behind himself.

"Pretty quiet," Alan told him. He was pretty, with blond hair and blue eyes. Classic beauty, but sometimes they didn't get enough appreciation. And Greyson was pretty sure he was only straight-acting. "Only a few people have booked the group class."

"Mmm." Greyson noticed the way Alan's gaze wandered down his sculpted biceps and toned forearms. He was more than used to people looking him over, and he was pretty damn sure this was a gay look rather than a look of admiration. "Quiet days are nice sometimes."

"Yeah. Less of a crowd in the gym. I might be able to sneak in a workout on my break," Alan grinned.

Greyson winked. "Let me know if you want a spotter."

A little smile flickered across Alan's lips. "Sure." They made eye contact for a few moments. Greyson pushed himself off the desk and Alan's eyes wandered down his body to his arms, watching them flex as Greyson pushed himself upright.

Alan's eyes flickered down to the raised white lines on the insides of his arms. Greyson nearly flinched but held firm.

Alan's eyes were back on his face, his smile a little more forced. "See you, then."

"See you around."

Greyson's jaw gritted as he strode off in that familiar measured pace, his hands instinctively going to tuck his thumbs into a utility belt that was no longer there. Without it, he didn't know where his confidence had gone, but it was shot.

Fuck. And his arms…

It was time to get this sorted once and for all. He'd been saving up for tattoos for *years*, and his skin had to be ready now.

At least he could find out whether it was or not.

He was gonna drop into the local tattoo shop. Yeah, it would be stupidly expensive, but it was also stupidly embarrassing. He'd always been better at hiding his insecurities than most, but it was damn near impossible to work out properly in a long-sleeved shirt.

And his arm hair *almost* covered the marks. Not enough, but almost.

Greyson grimaced and headed into the staff room to grab his water bottle and towel. Time to get ready for class.

CHAPTER
Three

FLOYD

"OH, FUCK, YOU'RE RIGHT. YOU WERE ONLY A GRADE AHEAD OF me, so my reunion's next year." Jackson leaned back in his chair with a groan. His boyfriend, Chase, laughed nearby at the dismayed expression he wore. "I suppose I have to go, since I'm living here..."

"Probably," Floyd laughed. "That's why I'm going, really. Otherwise I wouldn't bother."

"I wonder if anyone's traveling in."

"The popular kids would," Floyd snorted.

Jackson scoffed. "Yeah, like whatshisface, the soccer guy--"

"Ashton!" Floyd grimaced. What a dick. He'd always been a dick.

"Yeeeah. And the prom queens."

Floyd laughed. "Anyway, I'll probably be the sad, single gay guy there..."

"Not sad," Chase snorted. "You own your own fuckin' business. Most of them are probably stuck in unpaid internships."

Jackson winced as they all laughed. "Oooh, ouch."

"We could set you up with... someone..." Chase trailed off, looking at Jackson thoughtfully.

"Nah." Floyd couldn't think of anyone they knew that he didn't already know – their friendship circle was large but still tight-knit. They'd all gotten together for drinks just a few nights ago before one of his closest buddies from their group, Kevin, had moved. He'd left for Toronto to pursue his hockey career, and Floyd was missing the rough-and-tough, loyal, determinedly cheerful man.

At least Chase was still around, and though Chase was technically his employee at the tattoo shop, they were good friends. Which was why Chase was grinning at him. "Why not? Are you too shy?" he teased.

Floyd groaned and rolled his head back, refusing to let them embarrass him. "No."

"Do you prefer being single?" Jackson asked.

Floyd had to think about it for a few moments. That was a clever question, but difficult. Overall, though... "No. I'm not against dating."

"Well, if you'd prefer the hollow sentiments, let me know," Chase smiled.

Floyd chuckled. "I just see you guys all with your boyfriends..." he waved at Chase and Jackson, but he also meant Jackson's brothers. Jackson and his two brothers, Cam and Thomas, had bought three houses together, and within the first year of living there, they'd all found boyfriends who had moved in. The six of them seemed really happy now, and... it was easy to be jealous.

"My family's starting to lean on me," Floyd admitted. It was kind of a complicated story, but he could at least tell them that much. "Which is fuckin' ironic. They didn't want me around a few years ago, but now..." he trailed off, then cleared his throat.

Instantly, Floyd had a moment of guilt. He didn't talk shit about his family. The Rileys never did, so why should he? That just looked bad, and it wasn't who he wanted to be. The other two were silent, watching him with concerned expressions.

"Anyway, now that everything's going well for me, they want me settling down and stuff," Floyd concluded simply.

"You're worth being around in the good times and the bad," Chase told him softly. Jackson hummed his agreement, and Floyd's cheeks heated up.

"Thanks," Floyd brushed them off with a laugh. "I suppose I could do online dating."

Chase barely bit back a laugh, but then Jackson chuckled heartily.

Floyd felt like he was missing something. "What?"

"Nothing," Chase smirked. "Just... that's how we bonded."

"You didn't meet online!"

"No," Jackson laughed. "We were buddies, until I asked him for help with my dating profile..." His eyes gleamed mischievously. "So, who would you ask for help?"

"I don't – I don't have anyone in mind," Floyd laughed. "Maybe I'll just take a fake date."

"Ohhh. Oh man, that'd be fun," Jackson laughed. "If I didn't have a real date to take, I would."

"I was about to say--" Chase threatened, grabbing Jackson's collar playfully to draw him in while Jackson yielded.

Floyd laughed louder. "I'd have taken Kevin if he weren't fuckin' in Toronto now."

"I know, what a loser," Jackson sighed. "Cam's been moping around for days."

"Aww." Floyd rose to his feet to bring the dishes to the sink, but Chase interrupted to gather the dishes instead. "Okay, I should get to bed, guys. I'll have you over next time. I'm opening in the morning."

"Good luck. Think Kassie will remember the alarm?" Chase smirked.

"Fuckin' hope so," Floyd grumbled. He rubbed his face, then reached out to half-hug both his friends. "Thanks, guys."

"No problem. Let us know if we can help," Jackson said seriously while Chase nodded.

Floyd clapped Jackson's arm. "Thanks, man."

As he stepped into the warm street, he tucked his hands into his pockets for the short amble home. He only lived about a twenty-minute walk away, just on the other side of the downtown core, so he didn't mind it. In the summer months, it was actually enjoyable to get some fresh air on a warm evening. It was just winter that sucked here.

As he walked, he took his phone out of his pocket to flick through his messages and notifications. One of them was a badge on the Grindr icon.

Might as well have a look.

Floyd checked it, then snorted. Another message from an anonymous profile. He barely even glanced at it before discarding the idea, browsing through nearby matches instead.

"Oof," Floyd murmured. There *was* one new profile, but he didn't have a photo up yet. His stats were filled in, though – same age as him, similar kind of build. Without a photo, it was hard to know if there was much chemistry, or worse yet, if he already knew the guy.

He closed the app and pocketed his phone again, stretching as he wandered home through the evening. There were much less shady places to find an emergency date if it came to it later, anyway.

Still, walking home alone, away from the little group of houses holding his happily partnered friends, made Floyd's chest ache.

CHAPTER
Four

GREYSON

"Police are reporting a break-and-enter on the north side last night. A home on Main Street was broken into at around three AM last night. Police are advising citizens to keep their doors locked while investigations are ongoing."

Greyson's eyes narrowed as he pushed his hair back off his forehead. A break-and-enter? That wasn't very common here. They had the odd ones, sure, but usually it was people leaving their doors unlocked.

He still couldn't break the habit of morning radio. He ran around the neighborhood early every day, usually well before the sun was up in the winter. This time of year the sun was up, but few others were, so it was his favorite time to go for a run.

Gravel crunched under his feet as he turned onto the next street, enjoying having the sidewalk all to himself. There were a few dangerous spots without crosswalks where cars could suddenly turn, but he tried to avoid those when mapping out his routes.

He could always switch to the police scanner.

No, he told himself firmly. He had to break this habit. He wasn't going to get hired again – not after what had happened before. Not after Alberta, that was for damn sure.

Greyson slowed his pace as he switched his phone to playing music instead, settling into his usual morning jog playlist. Around the edges of his neighborhood, past the park, then through downtown, over the walking bridge and back to his own house. It took him a good forty minutes to an hour depending on how fit he felt each morning and how many times he stopped.

This routine was most important to him because of the endorphins. He needed that in the morning – it was the worst time for him, and the only thing that helped was an instant burst of happy hormones in his body.

Plus, he still woke up at stupidly early hours after nearly a decade of police work and irregular hours. The only thing to do at five AM was take up some useless hobby and start quilting or something. Browsing dating apps was out – nobody wanted a loser who was still awake at that hour, or someone so desperate to be discreet that he only signed in at that time.

He pivoted to avoid a pothole just in time, then let out a breath of relief. That would have been a nasty ankle twist. Fucking city was too broke to fix them, though.

Greyson wiped the sweat from his face as he took a moment at the red light, then crossed for the walking bridge. There were a few people out walking their dogs – two of them on the whole length of the bridge. He nodded to them and they both nodded back.

"And done," he breathed out as he reached the far end of the bridge, letting himself take a minute to turn around and start slowly walking back for a breather. God, the sun coming up over the river was beautiful some mornings. The trees were filling in, flush with leaves and tiny flowers. The dew on the grass was even romantic.

That was the other thing he missed – despite the hellish hours and the ugly sights sometimes, there were also moments of tranquility just sitting in the squad car watching the sun rise. Sometimes with his partner, sometimes alone.

He missed having a partner.

Greyson set off into another, quicker pace. He was going to push himself the whole way home.

———

"Hey, Darren, over here."

Greyson waved over his buddies – Darren and Lyle, his favorite guys from the department. They were still here even years later, both having worked their way up in seniority while he was off in Alberta.

Since coming back two months ago, he'd tried to hang out with them over breakfast every couple weeks. He just wanted to check in with them and get familiar with their lives again. So much had changed. They'd been mysteriously busy this week, though. They hadn't been texting back a lot.

"Hey," Lyle greeted, sliding in opposite him and nodding to the diner waitress for their usual. "How's it going?"

"Can't complain," Greyson answered, locking his fingers over his chest as he leaned back in the booth, his elbows out. "You two?"

"Good," they both answered automatically.

Greyson eyed them. "What happened?"

Darren seemed to hesitate, looking at Lyle first.

"Guys," Greyson said flat-out. "It's too early to bullshit me. What did you hear?"

"I... would rather hear it from you," Lyle said cautiously, shifting in his seat. His uniform stretched tight as he leaned back.

They all looked up and nodded in thanks to the waitress for pouring them coffee, then waited until she was out of earshot before exchanging looks again.

Greyson bit his lip hard, then nodded. "Okay." *I knew it was gonna come out sometime.* "We had this... domestic dispute. I was supposed to bring them both in. The department was getting stupid about that, about not knowing who was "really" at fault, even if that's bullshit."

They both nodded.

"I refused. It was... a gay couple."

Lyle started to look wary as he nodded. Between them hung the heavy memories, but none of them were touching *that*. They all remembered that night. Greyson had learned about Brett hitting Floyd, and he'd... taken matters into his own hands.

"One of them was pushing the other one around a lot. We'd gotten called twice before about them. The other one finally fought back. I wasn't gonna get him in shit for it. My supervisor disagreed and I... stood my ground."

"Ah." Darren nodded. "So they wanted you out?"

"Yeah. I quit, they fired me, whatever. Details. I wasn't welcome anymore," Greyson told them simply.

"That's... not all we heard."

Greyson's eyebrows rose with irritation and confusion. "What? What else is going around?"

"Nothin--" Lyle started, but Greyson leaned forward and frowned at him. "Fine. There's other... gayer rumors."

They couldn't know. Greyson hadn't come out to anyone here. Then again, he wasn't *hiding*. He just hadn't figured himself out until he'd moved to Alberta. And he sure as fuck didn't care what people here thought about it. "So? They not hiring gay cops these days? Is that back in fashion?" It came out a little more aggressively than he'd meant to.

Darren flinched. "No. Just... they're not a fan of work-place relationships."

Greyson reeled. *What kind of relationships?* That really *was* bullshit. He hadn't gotten involved with anyone even remotely connected to the department for exactly that reason. "I don't know. Those are rumors."

Lyle hummed and blew on his coffee. "Either way, they're as good as fact now. If you wanna get back in--"

"I don't."

"--you'll have to work harder."

Greyson's jaw twitched in irritation, but he clamped down on that sign of emotion and took a deep breath instead. Maybe people thought he'd been sleeping with one of those guys, or his supervisor, or the chief – who knew? Didn't make a difference.

Floyd... well, he'd heard enough after Floyd left to convince him he didn't want to be the gay cop. And there was only so much he'd been able to do to shut people up, especially from a precarious position like his.

"Right. Thanks for the heads-up," he finally settled on. "But fuck them all."

"Yeah," Darren nodded. "If you are... you know we're cool with it."

Greyson knew that. That was why he hung out with these two still. He offered a smile and quick nod. "Yeah. Thanks."

"But look out for yourself," Lyle added. "It's a lot friendlier here these days, but there's still assholes. You know, like..."

He didn't have to say it. Greyson's fists remembered him. "Yeah."

Their breakfast came and it broke the mood, letting them change the subject to better things: the B&E, a few bullshit calls lately, a house fire.

Afterward, he walked with Darren and Lyle back to their cruiser while they decided on a hockey game to go watch at the sports bar in a week or two. When they picked a game, Greyson memorized that date.

He didn't have a lot of friends right now, so he had to keep up with the few he had.

Greyson was surprised when Darren leaned in for a hand-clasping, back-patting quick hug, and then Lyle. *Fuck, did they see something?* He pulled down his sleeves once he leaned back again. He stretched out a lot of his shirts that way, but it was an unconscious habit more than anything.

"See you guys around. Be safe."

"You, too."

He watched them drive off, his heart heavy. He missed the force for the camaraderie more than anything. The department was a tight-knit family once you were in, and... well, that wasn't always a good thing.

Not remotely.

Greyson shivered, then redirected his thoughts to the new class as he climbed into his car for the drive home. He had to plan the next few weeks.

Five

FLOYD

"WELCOME," FLOYD GREETED AS THE SHOP DOOR RATTLED closed behind an average-build guy, three tattoos visible on his arms, maybe one on his leg. "Can I help you?"

"I'm looking for Chase's portfolio. I heard he works here?"

"Yeah, he does." Floyd was already rummaging for Chase's portfolio book. "Have you seen his work online?"

"Yeah."

"He has a few extra photos in here. Have you worked with him before?"

"Nope." The guy approached the counter. "Yeah, that's the guy. I saw those ones online."

Floyd flipped to the other photos – the stuff Chase couldn't post online. Just in case it got tracked back to him, and *other people* found him. He knew the truth now: that Chase's family was shitty and he'd moved here to get away from them, taking on almost a new identity. They'd found him, so now Chase was a little less fast and loose showing off his old work under his old name.

He'd worked hard over the last year to build up his new portfolio, and Floyd was damn proud of him.

"This is kind of like what I want." The guy pointed out a tattoo of a sailing boat. "That style for sure, and a yacht like this. That's what caught my eye."

"Oh, his style is perfect for that," Floyd nodded. "All right, sounds great. You wanna come in for a consultation?"

"Yeah, please. When's he in?"

"If you wanna come in at noon, he'll be around," Floyd told him. "He'll need some time to design for you since we do everything custom."

"That's fine."

"Okay, can I take your name?"

Floyd's mind wandered as he typed the appointment into the computer, taking down the new customer's details. Chase had been keeping busy over the last few months in particular, now that his portfolio was larger. Word of mouth was spreading and he was getting better business, not just more of it.

He'd come a long way since Floyd took the massive risk of hiring him with a portfolio he couldn't even show the public. The moment Floyd understood why that was, he'd been determined to keep Chase around until he could rebuild his career. He just hoped he wouldn't take off for bigger and better things now. At least having Jackson here ensured he was rooted in the city.

"All done. See you then," Floyd told the customer, Ricky.

Now to try to get himself some damn work.

Floyd didn't have to worry for long. Chase showed up just before noon, and by the time Floyd finished filling him in on the morning and on his customer, Ricky was back for his consultation.

While they talked in the back room, Floyd manned the front and sold some body jewelry. He had to kick out a teen who was obviously trying to get up the courage to ask for a tattoo without being ID'd, though.

Then the phone rang, and Floyd automatically answered. "Hello, Floyd here."

"Hi, I was wondering whether you take appointments."

"We do, and also walk-ins for consultations. We do custom designs only so we rarely do walk-in same-day tattoos, though. Did you want to talk to someone?"

There was a brief pause. "Ah, yeah... yes, I want to talk about some ideas first. See if they're possible." The voice sounded warm and familiar, but it wasn't the guy who called every now and then wanting something and never having the courage to actually get it done. He'd know *that* voice by now.

"Of course," Floyd answered. "Today works, come on in."

"Uh, first, what's your availability for actually doing it?"

"Well..." Floyd hedged. It was a bit of an open-ended question, really. "It depends on the complexity and how long it takes us to draw up the final design, how many hours the design takes... the first appointment in the next week is definitely possible. A sleeve or something will take weeks, a small piece can be done in one session, you know?"

"Right, right." The caller's voice sounded a little odd, but he cleared his throat. "Okay. Sure. I'll come in at six, if that's okay."

"What's your name, so I can make an appointment?"

"Peters."

He'd once known a Peters. Floyd's stomach twisted and he drew a breath. *Not that memory, please.* "Okay, thanks, man. See you at six."

After he hung up, Floyd rubbed his face. Of all the memories, he sure as hell didn't want to be lost in that one.

CHAPTER

Six

GREYSON

OH MAN, EGG SANDWICHES WERE GETTING OLD. THE PROTEIN shake was at least easier to change up by adding different flavors, but Greyson was going to have to find something else for his on-the-go post-workout meal.

Greyson leaned against the desk in the back room as he ate, his mind going over the class. A few slow students today, but they were new. He'd have to adapt their exercises a little next class if they were still having trouble. One of them seemed to have a lot more fun than the other, though.

"How's it goin'?" It was Jake, one of the other instructors. He'd been running a spin class at the same time.

Greyson swallowed and shrugged. "Can't complain. You?"

"Good, good." Jake grabbed his towel and dumped his water bottle off in his locker. "Holy shit, that was a bad class."

Greyson winced in sympathy. "How so?"

"Just... you know... one of those days. Got started late, a few people had trouble, one person nearly fell off her bike..."

Greyson almost choked on his sandwich. "How?"

"She had the seat loosened. I caught it in time, but only

21

just. It wasn't as dramatic as it sounded, but you know. Little things add up."

Greyson punched Jake's arm lightly. "We all got those days."

"Yeah. Coming to the shower?"

"In a sec." Greyson waved the rest of his shake, then tipped his head back to drink it.

"Still loading up on the protein? Don't think you have enough muscles now, big guy?" Jake grinned. "Are you going for a Mike look?"

Mike was the gym rat here. The guy hogged the plates from dawn 'til dusk. He came in at least twice a day and for an hour each time. They were all pretty sure he didn't have a girlfriend or a job.

"Fuck, no."

Mike was really, grossly fit. Like the kind of over-muscled type that screamed "I only eat steak and eggs for breakfast, lunch, and supper" and made clothes shopping impossible. Worse yet, the kind of muscle that looked great but couldn't lift a handcuffed suspect and haul him into the back of a squad car on demand.

Greyson's style was fit, compact, and action-based. He wanted to be able to *do* shit, not just look like he could.

Jake snorted with laughter and headed for the men's showers. The center was small enough that the instructors had their own back room, but not their own shower room.

Of all the things Greyson wanted, that was probably number one. His own shower space, so he didn't have to see men's naked asses all over the place. Not that wasn't what he was into, but precisely *because* that was what he was into.

He drew a breath and steeled his nerves, then grabbed his towel and gym bag. He ducked through the opposite hallway door into the men's locker room and regretted once again his choice to take a class during one of the most popular times of day.

Most of the guys minded their own business, and he knew as well as them how to. He kept his eyes averted from theirs, found a spot for his bag, and stripped off for the shower, dumping his old clothes in one half of his bag. Towel around his waist, he headed for the crappy '70s-esque tiled group shower. He'd seen showers like this in more porn clips than he could count.

"Hey," Jake jerked his chin when he noticed Greyson passing. Greyson hadn't even seen him, too busy being careful not to look either at eye level or waist level.

"Hey." Greyson shoved his towel across the bar and turned on the water, shivering until it got hot. That helped keep his nerves cold, at least. "When's your next class?"

"Tomorrow, the advanced spin class."

Greyson soaped up quickly. "What, you gonna teach them to do a wheelie?" he shot back across the sound of water. A couple other guys were chatting in that same "we're all naked but nothing's gay about this" casual tone.

Jake groaned. "I've never heard that one before."

Greyson snorted with laughter. "I never said I had a sense of humor. I don't think they asked for that on the job application."

"Damn it. I should get them to add that." Jake turned off his shower and scrubbed his hair and face with the towel before wrapping it around his waist again. "I'm subbing for someone on Tuesday, I think they said."

"Bet I know who that was." Greyson sighed. One of the newer instructors, Kyle, wasn't the most responsible. He was gonna end up doing Kyle's core strength classes again next week at this rate.

"Yeah, Kyle keeps taking bookings for one-on-one sessions at the same time as his group classes." Jake strode out to the locker area again.

That was just basic stupidity, then. They got paid much better for group classes assuming the group was more than a couple people. Kyle seemed really forgetful, though. It was probably just not looking at his calendar closely enough. "Huh." Greyson turned off his shower and scrubbed off fast, avoiding looking at the other six or seven guys in the showers on the way out.

Jake was on the other side of the benches, so Greyson turned his back to him as he changed into his new outfit. "Sounds shitty. If you need me to take a class or two, I don't have a life, so..."

Jake laughed. If Greyson remembered right, he had too much of a life, so he'd be grateful for the help. He was the guy with two almost-girlfriends, after all.

"Yeah, things are getting complicated."

Greyson snorted. "Like they weren't already."

"One of them wants to take me to her cabin for a hot weekend. I'm liking the other one more, though. I think she wants to actually date me."

Greyson rolled his eyes. "Gotta pick one, dude. I keep telling you."

"But what if I pick the wrong one?" Jake tossed his towel across his bag, drawing Greyson's attention for a moment. Jake was buttoning up his jeans.

Christ, the man had abs. Greyson tried to keep his eyes on Jake's face now, and not the bulges of his arms or his toned stomach. That was the problem: every instructor here was hot, and he couldn't bang any of them. For multiple reasons.

"Well..." Greyson helplessly raised his shoulders. "You tell the other one you need to think about shit, I don't know." *It's a lot easier with guys.* "You're asking the wrong guy."

Jake paused for a moment in the middle of pulling his shirt on, that perceptive flash of realization dawning on him.

Jesus. I could have taken that a different direction. Greyson didn't take back his comment, though. He raised his shoulders in a shrug. "I'm not the love guru. I just think it's a bad idea if one of them can find out about the other... at best, you're gonna hurt one of them. Better sooner than later."

"Right, right," Jake agreed, the moment passing as he pulled his shirt down. To his credit, he didn't act any different. "I know what I have to do."

"Then do it, man." Greyson buttoned up his shirt, pulling the sleeves down properly and running a hand over his hair.

Jake nodded. "Whatcha doing today? We should grab a drink sometime."

The tension drained out of Greyson's shoulders. That was a hand of friendship – unless he was some closet case trying to work out his issues on him. *Again.* "Sure," he agreed. "I can't do today, but sometime soon, for sure."

"Great," Jake smiled.

When Greyson glanced toward the door, he saw Alan writing on the whiteboard just inside the door. He was putting down the class schedule for the week. "Hey."

Alan glanced at them both and nodded, his gaze flickering between the two of them. Then it cleared up. "Ah, you both just had class, huh?"

"Don't even ask," Greyson laughed.

Alan winced and nodded. "Right, right." He looked more at Jake than Greyson. "Just put down the new class here."

Greyson scanned the board. It was another damn kettle bell class, of course. "Who's doing it?"

"Kyle."

Greyson went to swap looks with Jake, but Jake was rolling his eyes at Alan.

"Right." Greyson shook his head, then shouldered his gym bag. They couldn't publicly bitch about him, but he so wanted to.

Alan awkwardly smiled and raised a hand, then ducked out of the gym room again. Just before he did, his eyes fell to Greyson's arms. It was an unmistakable glance.

Greyson resisted the urge to flinch. *Fuck. I wasn't wrong. These tattoos better make a difference.*

CHAPTER
Seven

FLOYD

The door bell jangled and Floyd looked up with an automatic welcoming smile.

Oh, holy fuck. No way. Not *that* Peters... Not Greyson Peters.

It was.

"H-Hey," Floyd managed, his hands curling into tight fists below the counter as he shifted his stance.

Greyson was staring right back at him, standing stock-still in the entrance right in front of the door. He looked just as surprised to be walking back into Floyd's world again.

And Greyson was hot now.

Holy shit, was he ever. Greyson was chiseled and muscled, the baby face dropping away from his cheekbones and scruff wandering down his neck. His lips looked as soft as ever, but there was a darker air about his eyes. The years had aged Greyson a little faster than Floyd.

Greyson had the lean kind of strength that came with their job. No, Greyson's job... not Floyd's anymore.

As Greyson set into motion toward the counter with a

shaky smile of greeting, he walked like a man now – self-assured but not overeager, like a green recruit wanting to prove himself everywhere he went in the world.

He looked calmer now, quieter, more introspective.

Christ, that was all bullshit. Floyd hadn't even talked to the man yet, but his mind was getting away from him.

"Long time no see," Floyd nodded. Just seconds had passed, but under Greyson's intense scrutiny, it felt like so much longer. Like years.

Shit. All those years ago... Greyson had been right. Did he know that now?

Greyson's eyes were locked on his now, and Floyd couldn't look away. "Years, yeah." His voice was warm but deeper now, the timbre deep in his chest making Floyd's fingers tingle.

"Do you-- We should go out for coffee sometime." *What the fuck? No, shut up,* Floyd reprimanded himself. The guy might well hate him now. After what had happened...

"Yeah."

"You guys go catch up." That was Chase, and Floyd nearly jumped out of his skin. "Whoa, sorry," Chase laughed, holding up his hands in a peace gesture as he leaned in the hallway. "I can mind the shop as long as you need. I'm done with my appointments."

"Thanks," Floyd murmured. There was no way he was seeing this guy for a consultation without saying...

Saying what?

Sorry? Glad to see you again? I want to bang you like a screen door in a hurricane, so are you still straight?

Floyd's thoughts were racing and damn near impossible to control. "Just gonna grab my keys..." he mumbled, ducking into the office to do that and get a moment to himself.

Greyson was not giving him a straight vibe anymore. Not even remotely. And he wasn't giving him anything to read in body language or emotions – probably because they weren't alone.

Floyd had no idea what to expect, and it was a terrifying thrill.

What the hell was this reaction? And what was Greyson doing back here after all this time? He'd never find out if he didn't calm the fuck down.

He let out a breath and grabbed his keys, then turned to the office door again.

Time to face the music.

CHAPTER
Eight
GREYSON

THE SMELL OF SAMOSAS, HOT DOGS, AND PIZZA FROM NEARBY restaurants wafted through the air, making Greyson lick his lips. Now that he thought about it, he wouldn't mind a bite to eat.

Worse yet, the smell of cigarette smoke. Jesus fuck, he wished he hadn't quit smoking last year. He only had a craving once every few months at most now. He couldn't remember the last time he'd wanted one – but he couldn't remember the last time he'd been under this kind of pressure.

What the fuck was he going to do or say? How did Floyd end up behind the counter there, muscled and tattooed and looking like a man who took no shit?

Most important: why did Greyson *want* him so much? Floyd had softer eyes now than before, and a quicker smile. His lips were full and pink and perfect, and his jeans were tight around his muscled thighs, and...

No. This was a tangent. Greyson had recognized the

voice on the phone, but thought *no way could it be the same Floyd Turner*. Apparently he was wrong.

Greyson let out a breath. As long as his ex-patrol partner hadn't gotten back together with Brett. If he had, surely he wouldn't even want to talk to him.

Greyson slipped a hand into his pocket as he leaned against the stone wall, then pinched his thigh as hard as he could.

That bled off a little of his tension, letting him breathe out a deep sigh. He breathed in again and straightened up as the shop door jangled.

"Hey."

"Hi," Floyd answered. He seemed to be over his shock now, lightly smiling as he joined Greyson on the sidewalk.

Fuck, he was gorgeous now. He was built broader than Greyson, as he'd always been, and he had a short-sleeved t-shirt on to show off tattoo sleeves all the way up his arms. There was no doubt he was a tattoo artist – no piercings, so he wasn't a piercer. What did his hands feel like running over bare skin? Holy shit, he'd soon find out.

"You own that place?"

"Yeah."

"Wow," Greyson hummed. "I – had no idea, man. Coffee. How about, uh..." he nodded down the street to the cafe a few doors away.

"Sure." Floyd set off into a gentle amble, looking Greyson up and down. "You still a cop?" Their history as patrol partners was still fresh in his mind, too, then.

Greyson winced. "No." He cleared his throat, scratching at his stubble. "Uh, no. Not anymore. I quit a couple months back. Moved back here."

"Ahh. I hadn't heard. Or seen you around, I guess."

"No," Greyson nodded. "I'm a fitness instructor right now."

Floyd nodded, holding open the door for Greyson to walk through.

Greyson's cheeks heated up but he stepped through with a quick, jerky nod. "Been here before? I haven't."

"All the time. I work right there," Floyd gently reminded him with a teasing grin.

Duh. Don't say stupid shit. "Oh," Greyson laughed. "Uh, yeah. What's good here?"

"Everything. I like the lattes."

"Latte it is."

They grabbed coffees, each paying for their own and leaving the change, then took them to a corner table. Floyd asked for it to go, so Greyson did, too. The whole time, they carefully maintained a distance of a few feet, glancing at each other now and again. It felt like a first date.

Only once they were tucked in the corner did Floyd's shoulders relax a little as he leaned back to take Greyson in as Greyson did exactly the same.

"Right. So, I... own that place now," Floyd explained after a moment. "After stuff happened, I decided I should be a tattoo artist. I sort of stumbled into the ownership bit."

Greyson nodded. *Stuff happened?* He couldn't ask, though.

"I went off the rails," Floyd explained concisely. "I had my epiphany and made a go of it. I got into competitive archery, got a little more confidence, and wound up here."

"Ohhh." Greyson winced. "Did you... uh, I mean, was it...?"

"You can say his name. Brett. No. I broke up with him right after you left."

Horrible as it sounded, Greyson had never been more thankful.

"Oh, good--"

"Thanks to you."

Greyson knew his cheeks were burning. He opened his mouth, then gave a sheepish little laugh. "That's not... I know I fucked up before."

"So did I."

Greyson hesitated, then reached out a hand across the table. Floyd didn't hesitate to take it, and Greyson's nerves crackled with electricity at the warm touch of the firm palm against his own. "We're good?"

"Good."

They pumped hands once, and Greyson was surprised to find how breathless he felt once Floyd let go.

He wanted that hand on him... somewhere else. Anywhere else.

Oh, Jesus, he was gonna get hard if he didn't think of something else fast. Not the moment.

"I listened to you, years too late," Greyson laughed quietly. "That's how I ended up quitting or being driven out, doesn't really matter. I'm not really welcome there anymore. So I'm back here doing fitness classes, and... that's kinda nice. I know a lot about it."

"Yeah, you always did," Floyd nodded. "I'm sorry that happened."

Greyson smiled. "Thanks. It's all right. I prefer this life anyway. Pension's crap, but the hours are better."

Floyd laughed, the first genuine smile spreading across his face as Greyson grinned at him. "Actually," Floyd added, "I've been meaning to pick up some kind of sport. I do pushups at home and shit, but nothing proper. I dropped archery after last season. Got bored, I guess."

"You should come along," Greyson instantly invited him.

"Group class or one-on-one. It's great. I work at the Y. I'll get those arms trained up again."

Floyd smiled broadly. "I'd like that."

"God, it's so weird," Greyson laughed quietly. "You haven't changed a bit, and yet... you know, suddenly tattooed all over..."

"It wasn't that sudden," Floyd laughed. "Might be for you – you still walk like a cop."

Greyson rolled his eyes, but he knew it was true. He admired how Floyd had utterly cut it out of his whole behavior – he slouched and sprawled, his arm along the back of the chair next to his. He ambled instead of striding, hands in his pockets instead of at the ready.

He'd been quick to leave the force, after all.

"I got this one two years after I quit, and it was my first." Floyd pulled his t-shirt sleeve up to show a bear paw etched across his shoulder. It was intricately woven into the top of his tattoo sleeve now.

"Right," Greyson laughed. "They all look great. Speaking of which..."

Floyd's eyes lit up. "Right! The consultation. We should do that in the shop so I can sketch and stuff. Take this with us?"

Greyson took his cup and stood up, shouldering his way out from the corner first and leading them back to the shop. He could swear he felt Floyd's eyes flicker down to his ass, but maybe that was just wishful thinking.

CHAPTER
Nine

FLOYD

"Okay," Floyd cracked his knuckles once they were settled in the back room. He'd hoped taking Greyson to his work space instead of the place he'd taken three of his first dates in the last couple years would make him focus.

It really didn't.

Greyson's forearms were still rippling distractingly under his long sleeves, his pecs rounding under his shirt in ways that made Floyd want to rub them.

He was *hot* for his former partner. That was fucking weird.

"I'm looking for..." Greyson unbuttoned his shirt, then hesitated two buttons down, his cheeks suddenly scarlet. "Oh, do you min--"

"No," Floyd quickly interrupted, waving him on. "I mean, yeah, go on."

Greyson *had* flirted with him once or twice back then, Floyd was sure of it. Maybe just in that casual way that meant he was comfortable in his sexuality... but maybe not. Now Floyd was starting to think he'd been gay all along.

"Arm? Shoulder?" Floyd asked.

"Arms, both of them. Sleeves."

Floyd whistled. Did he have others? From a quick glance at his bare torso and chest – bare and *ripped*, Jesus Christ – it didn't look like it. "Starting with sleeves? Normally I won't do that."

"I know," Greyson sighed. "I've just been saving up for these rather than doing them in pieces."

"Right." Floyd nodded, glancing quickly at those rippling biceps. "Full sleeves? You've got lots of skin to work with." *Work mode. Strictly work mode, please,* he begged himself. He didn't want to think about how much he wanted to straddle those hot thighs and grind himself against Greyson's hot stomach...

"Yeah. I know it's expensive."

"That was gonna be my first thing," Floyd laughed, focusing once again on Greyson's eyes.

The chemistry between them was so intense he could have cut it with a knife. Surely to God Greyson felt that, too.

Greyson nodded once. "I wanna go from about here," he gestured along his shoulder, "down to the wrist."

"The full length? Okay. Do you have designs in mind?"

"Well... did you do your own ones?"

Floyd immediately pointed out the parts of his forearms that he'd done himself. "It was a real bitch to do on myself, but yeah, all of that is mine. That isn't. This is..."

As he pointed out his own work, woven amongst other artists', Greyson's eyes followed his finger, and he absent-mindedly licked his lips.

He has to feel it.

"Okay. That's a lot like the style I want."

"Perfect," Floyd grinned. "Like you planned it."

"What? No. No, I had no idea it was you," Greyson scoffed, and Floyd raised his eyebrows at the defensive moment. Instantly, Greyson chuckled it off. "Sorry. I just didn't want you to think I was stalking you or something."

Floyd smirked. "Don't worry. I can look after myself." *These days a lot more than back then.* A shiver ran down his spine and he focused again on Greyson here and shirtless in front of him, not struggling under his hands to punch his boyfriend one more time...

Telling Brett he didn't deserve Floyd.

Now, Floyd knew he'd been right.

"I – um, the thing is, I don't know if I can get it done over these."

Greyson flipped his inner arms over to show Floyd, his expression suddenly steely. White scars crossed his forearms from side to side, some angular and some deeper than others.

Floyd had long since trained the reaction out of himself. He'd seen scars of all kinds and tattooed over them. It was surprisingly common in all ages, but especially younger people. Guys his own age and younger.

"Let's see. The only important thing is if they're old enough."

"Six, seven months."

Floyd took a step closer to Greyson, who was still sitting on the tattoo chair with his arms facing up. "Can I...?"

Greyson nodded, and Floyd wrapped one hand around the underside of one of his forearms to steady it while he ran his finger down the lines. They didn't feel that bad, compared to some he'd seen. He'd worked on worse.

Greyson's arm hair tickled against his fingertips, and a muscle twitched under his touch. They were close – close enough that Floyd could swear he felt Greyson's breath against his chest.

Floyd stepped back and let go of Greyson's arm, his body still crackling with the tension. "Yeah, I can do them as long as there's nothing fresh."

Greyson jerkily nodded. "There won't be."

"Then yeah, I can." Floyd *was* surprised, despite his professionalism. Greyson, of all people? He'd never seen that in him. Mind you, it was always the people you didn't expect. He just hoped Greyson was getting help for that shit.

"Good." Greyson looked so relieved Floyd wanted to punch his shoulder and tease him, just to break the tension. "I was thinking gray ink, actually. Dot work, if I can. Angel wing feathers from here to down to here... blending into nature scenery around the, uh... forearms..." *Around the scars,* Floyd thought as Greyson finished, "I think that'd look nice."

"That'd be kickass," Floyd agreed, his mind already spinning with designs as he got a good look at Greyson's arms. There was so much muscle there that he had a pretty big canvas to work with. "I need a bit of time to sketch this up, though."

"Yeah, of course."

"How about you come back..." Floyd pulled his phone out. "Right, it's Tuesday..."

"Forgetting your days of the week?" Greyson laughed. He pulled his shirt back on, quickly buttoning up again. That made it easier to focus, at least.

"Shut up," Floyd laughed. "Come back Friday. Friday evening? You working?"

"No, that's fine. I'd work before that. My classes are pretty much every day, actually," Greyson told him. "Sunday's my day off, though."

Floyd smiled. "Yeah? Cool. Friday evening. So, tattoo-wise, if you want this done fast, we can do sessions every Friday."

"That's fine," Greyson quickly answered. "That's perfect."

Floyd smiled, then punched Greyson's arm lightly. "Awesome."

"Thanks." Greyson pushed himself to his feet, and there was an awkward moment where they took each other in. Was this a handshake? A hug? A hand-clasp?

Floyd gripped Greyson's hand and shook it firmly, then leaned in for a half-hug. "It's great to see you again, man," he said, and he meant it.

Greyson relaxed and clapped his back in return. "You, too." He was smiling again, just like the old days. That darkness had lifted for a moment, his eyes sparkling. "Even if you've bulked out. Fuckin' unfair. You always gained so much easier." Floyd hadn't had to lift as hard as Greyson to get the same gains, and he'd gotten lazy.

"I like to challenge you," Floyd smirked, letting go of Greyson's hand and opening the door to walk him out. "You're welcome."

"Jesus," Greyson snorted. "I'd like to see you *try*."

Floyd jerked his chin. "Maybe I will," he laughed. He had no idea how well he'd do in a gym, but he could certainly try.

It would mean spending more time around Greyson again. He suddenly remembered all those long hours spent just quietly sitting in the cold patrol car together. His mind, his heart, and his dick were all in agreement that he wanted more of that again. He just had to figure out which of those things won out.

"See you Friday."

As the shop door swung closed, Floyd felt Chase's eyes on him. He'd never been more thankful for anything when Chase didn't ask, and just let him head to the back room to wipe down the chair and grab his sketch book.

Floyd wouldn't have known how to answer yet.

CHAPTER

Ten

GREYSON

G REYSON WAS ALMOST SHAKING FROM ADRENALINE AND nerves.

When he'd called for a consultation, that voice had sounded familiar, but he hadn't suspected it in the slightest. Floyd, of all people, working at some sketchy tattoo place?

Well, not *that* sketchy... it was actually pretty clean and bright. Nowhere near as sketchy as the other one he'd checked out.

But this was exactly what he needed: tattoos to keep him from relapsing. The temptation was still there, crawling under his skin, and the last six months had been fucking hard-fought.

Greyson ignored the voice in the back of his mind that reminded him he hadn't always won that battle. He'd just kept his arms clean. His thighs were always a safe bet.

"Jesus," he whispered under his breath, rubbing his face. He could use a meal and a drink, just to ground him after that experience.

Seeing Floyd again...

He was still unmistakably gay. This time, Greyson was willing to admit to himself that he was, too.

That didn't mean anything had to happen. But what did it mean that he *wanted* it to?

Greyson chose a pub nearby and ate at the bar, barely noticing anyone around him. Fish and chips was exactly what he wanted right now – fat and salt and vinegar.

Best of all, a nice cold beer.

"Hey."

It was Greyson's turn to nearly jump out of his skin. He'd almost laughed at how Floyd had let himself be snuck up on earlier, but then he went and did the same damn thing.

One of the guys he knew from high school... a year below him, if he remembered right. Jackson Riley. Everyone from high school seemed to be back here these days.

Oh yeah! Jackson was the gay blacksmith. What a combination.

Greyson shifted and reached out a hand to shake hard. "Hey, Jackson, right? Long time no see."

"You too. You living back here or what?"

Greyson nodded. "I've been back a couple months now. I think I'm gonna spend a few years here. Who knows?"

"Yeah? Cool," Jackson smiled. "You doing good? You're a cop, huh?"

"Was. Out in Alberta. Back here teaching classes at the Y now."

"Oh yeah?" Jackson smiled. "If I needed more of a workout I'd hit you up," he laughed. "But..."

"You're the blacksmith, aren't you? I heard about you," Greyson nodded. "Kinda hard not to."

"The gay blacksmith," Jackson corrected him with a roll of his eyes. He saw right through that attempt to be polite.

Greyson laughed. "That too, maybe." The town was damn small, after all. Ever since finding out he was gay – by way of his relationship status on Facebook back in Alberta – his mother had filled him in on the gay men in town. She was nosy, so he felt like he knew them all already.

If rumor was right, it wasn't just Jackson who was gay, either. "Are your brothers...?"

"Yep," Jackson laughed. "You heard about them, too, huh?"

Greyson shrugged. "My mom was always nosy."

Jackson snorted, then gestured over at the table. "We're all having drinks right now, actually. You wanna join us?"

Greyson wasn't sure what kind of company he'd be. Not with this restless itch of pent-up tension crawling under his skin.

But it would be rude to say no.

"Sure." Greyson pushed back his empty plate and grabbed his beer, following Jackson over to the table.

There were already half a dozen other guys sitting around the table, and Greyson recoiled with surprise. He didn't remember their family being *that* large.

He vaguely recognized Cam, mostly because he looked a bit like his older brother.

"Hey, guys. This is Greyson. He was in the year above me, and I think we got stuck together in one of those shitty grade 11-12 mixed psychology classes..."

Greyson laughed. He'd forgotten about that. "Yeah, we did. Hi."

No, he recognized a couple of these guys. Cam was definitely the hockey player. He'd seen the artsy-looking one somewhere around, and maybe one of the others. Small towns.

One by one, he met Cam and Thomas, Jackson's brothers, and their boyfriends Noah and Alex respectively.

"And this is my boyfriend, Chase..."

He was tattooed, too, but he looked a little more feminine than Floyd. A lot more, actually. "Hi."

"And Ryan, who we've adopted. He's a buddy of ours."

Greyson laughed and nodded. "Hey."

"Okay, that's everyone, until Floyd gets here." Greyson must have looked stunned, because Jackson glanced at him. "You know him? Oh yeah, he'd be about your age."

"We... know each other, yeah," Greyson laughed, trying to keep it casual now. "I just went in to see him today, actually."

"Oh, at work?" Chase asked.

"He's Chase's boss."

Small *fucking* towns.

"No way," Greyson laughed. "Yeah, for tattoos. He's drawing up some designs."

"Awesome," Chase approved. He punched Jackson's shoulder. "This guy got one of mine."

"Several of yours, I think," Jackson smirked, the innuendo clear. They pecked lips while Cam rolled his eyes and Thomas snorted.

"Jesus," Noah laughed, looking at Greyson instead. "So you work around here?"

Greyson nodded. "At the YMCA. I teach fitness classes."

"Oh, yeah? What kind?"

"Every kind, mostly strength conditioning and core strength and weight machines. I don't really go in for spin," Greyson chuckled.

Noah frowned. "Oh, those are my favorites."

"We'll get you lifting more than a peanut butter jar some-day," Cam teased.

"Don't need to. I have you for that." Noah grinned cheekily at Cam, then looked back at Greyson. "Sorry. Ryan's always saying it gets a bit much being out with us."

"Yeahhh," Ryan groaned, swigging his beer as Greyson laughed. "They supply me with booze though."

"That's what friends are for."

"Oh, hey, Floyd – guess who we picked up?" Jackson grinned.

Greyson turned to see Floyd approaching, and as they made eye contact, Floyd's jaw dropped. "No way. You're everywhere suddenly," Floyd said.

"Sorry," Greyson laughed, not sure yet if that was a bad thing or not. He was half-ready to leave.

"No, no. Don't go." Floyd sounded a bit too quick to say that, which was intriguing.

Greyson settled down and nodded, letting Floyd pull up another chair next to him instead as they all scooted over.

"Just ate?" Floyd asked.

"Yeah. Have you?"

Floyd smiled. "I grabbed a bite before I came."

Their shoulders almost brushed with so many of them crammed around the table, but Greyson made himself focus on anything but that. "So you know all these guys?"

"I somehow got roped into it, yeah," Floyd laughed. "I hired Chase, and then one thing led to another..."

"And we decided we'd keep him," Alex grinned. "Actually, no, he was around before me..."

"He was. You're the newcomer. Shush, newcomer."

Alex groaned. "I've been the newcomer for months now. Technically, I've known Thomas--"

"Newcomer," Jackson and Cam said simultaneously to

drown him out, and Greyson laughed heartily. Alex gave them the middle finger.

Even though it was mostly family members around the table, the atmosphere was warm and welcoming. He couldn't remember the last time he'd sat in this big a group of men and not felt... weird about it, in one way or another.

It was easy to relax into a few beers with the group. They talked sports, beer, and weather.

When the conversation hit Alberta, though, at least Greyson had a few things to offer. "Things are getting rough there. A lot of guys getting laid off."

"Yeah, some of them are coming back home," Jackson nodded seriously.

Thomas clicked his tongue. "None of them saved up what they made. I see it at the bank, too. You make a six-figure income, you should have a damn house within a couple years. But they blow it on sex and drugs..."

"Not even worthwhile stuff, like art," Noah muttered. *That* was where Greyson had seen him – some art gallery show he'd gone to with a blind date. Everyone laughed at that reaction. "What?"

"Nothing. You're right," Cam smiled, hugging Noah around the shoulders before looking back at Greyson. "So you worked out there or what?"

"Yeah, as a cop."

"Ooof." Several of them were wincing sympathetically already while Floyd leaned back a little to watch him.

Greyson nodded tightly. "There's some... messed-up shit that happens when you give a bunch of stupid young guys a lot of money and nowhere to spend it."

But however many drunken bar fights he'd gone to, it was nothing compared to the domestic violence cases.

Like *that* one. The fucker. It still made his blood boil.

"Glad to be back here, then, huh?" That was Floyd, his voice soft and understanding. Greyson almost cringed at the knowledge that he knew exactly how deeply some of those memories had imprinted on him.

"Yeah."

Cam cleared his throat. "Here's to that." They all toasted Greyson, whose cheeks burned with embarrassment as he lifted his beer to clink with theirs.

"To Fredericton," Greyson agreed. What a phrase to toast to. He'd never thought he'd hear *that* one.

A few beers later, everyone was more relaxed, and Floyd was only looking hotter.

Damn it, it was hard to stay focused with Floyd right in his peripheral vision, his eyes attentive and his arms folded along the table in front of him. His lashes were still long, framing those pretty eyes. He was built solid, though – the kind of guy Greyson would wrestle into bed.

Christ, the thought made his dick twitch. Why the fuck was he thinking of his old partner naked and gasping his name? He needed to get laid.

Jackson's raised voice made Greyson flinch with surprise, his cheeks burning. Had he just been too obvious? But it wasn't that. "Okay, Floyd's almost done," Jackson laughed.

Greyson grinned. "We're *all* done, I think."

Floyd pushed himself to his feet. "I'm fine, but yeah, I gotta get home. Work and all."

"I'll go with you," Cam started to offer, but Greyson shook his head.

"I'll go. We can talk more about the tattoo designs anyway. I had a couple more ideas."

Floyd lit up. "I'll talk tattoos all night."

"I know he will," Chase groaned into his beer, prompting another round of laughter. "Good luck with him."

Greyson snorted and raised a hand to wave to the guys. "Thanks, guys. See you all around."

He and Floyd picked their way around tables and out of the stiflingly warm pub. It had been ages since he'd enjoyed himself so much. He tried not to think about why that might be, but Floyd was just... right there.

"Back this way," Floyd told him. "Still the same apartment. Where do you live?"

"Same way, in a house. Close to where... Jesus, you haven't moved? In, like, *a decade?*"

"Rent's good."

Greyson laughed. "Wow. It must be." Floyd's place was vaguely familiar to him – he'd been over a couple times when they were the newest cops, getting to know each other as partners on and off the job. It had been a damn nice little apartment in a downtown building.

He walked with Floyd past the dark shops and brightly-lit bars until they got to the edge of downtown, then crossed to the residential streets. Neither of them said much along the way, just enjoying the buzz of a few drinks and a lot of laughter. They exchanged numbers, and Greyson's heart fluttered with pleasure that he got to have Floyd's number again.

"I'm glad you came out," Floyd finally spoke up.

Greyson's lips twitched. "Me, too. And came here tonight."

Floyd's eyebrows shot up, and he started to laugh. "Dude."

Well, that wasn't subtle. Greyson snorted, too, then joined in Floyd's laughter. "Yeah..." They crossed the street, still laughing.

When Floyd's surprise settled, he peered at him. "I always wondered."

Greyson shrugged. "Yeah. I was confused or whatever."

"I'm glad," Floyd nodded, his voice simple and sincere. Then, he cleared his throat. "Not that you were confused back then, but that you're better now--"

"Yeah, I know. I'm glad too."

Greyson still remembered the moment he'd learned a tough guy like Floyd actually went home to another man. It had been like a wakeup call, but one he'd slept through as long as possible. In Alberta, surrounded by hot young men and not much else, it had finally been impossible to ignore.

"You look good now," Floyd added. "Happier?"

"Yeah. Definitely. So do you," Greyson told him. They were approaching Floyd's apartment, and his stomach twisted with this regret. This conversation was *almost* getting somewhere...

"Thanks. I sure as hell am, too."

They stopped outside Floyd's building door, facing each other now. Floyd's hair was pushed back, his eyes hazy from the same drinks Greyson felt tingling through his hands.

It might have been the alcohol, or the quiet night around them pushing them together like they'd been planning it all along.

Either way, they rocked forward, hands grasping each other's shoulders for brief moments, eyes closing and lips touching...

Lips pressing hard, wet, and warm. Sliding, caressing each other's, kissing like they were born to it. Floyd took a step forward and Greyson's hand ran down his spine to the small of his back as they kissed with desperate, tiny gasps for breath.

Then Floyd's eyes flew open at the same moment's as Greyson as the impulsive moment gave way to realization.

They were kissing.

Shit.

Greyson's cheeks paled as Floyd stared at him, neither of them willing to quite acknowledge that moment, even if they both seemed to sway slightly with the impulse to step closer again.

"See you."

"Bye."

Floyd disappeared inside and Greyson stayed there for a minute more, his lips still parted as his chest pounded. That... That shouldn't have felt so heavenly.

That was chemistry, plain and simple. The kind that made him want to jump into bed with Floyd, undress him, see what they had in common these days. The kind that made his head spin with desire. The kind that... made him want to do really impulsive, stupid shit.

That was impulsive *and* stupid.

Don't kiss your ex-partner. Especially that *ex-partner. Isn't that rule one?*

And... Friday. They were still on for Friday. Greyson couldn't avoid Floyd for long.

CHAPTER
Eleven

FLOYD

SINCE GOING STONE-COLD SOBER, FLOYD GOT HANGOVERS really easily... especially off beer. But Floyd didn't regret this hangover for a second.

He wasn't sure he would have ever got the courage to kiss Greyson without a couple beers in them both. Then again, doing it that way meant he didn't know if Greyson's interest extended past a couple beers and walking him home.

On Friday, when they saw each other, he had to sort this out.

He couldn't slip back into this habit. Drinking wasn't going to cure a damn thing – he'd learned that years ago, after all. It might have been a social lubricant, but for their second interaction, he couldn't let that happen again.

In the meantime, he had his headache and stomach ache to take care of, and then he had to get himself adjusted to light, and then... ready to drive.

"Fuck."

He had to drive his mother around shopping today, of all

things. Floyd rubbed his eyes and then his face, slowly rolling out of bed for the shower. A shower would help.

This was far from the first time he'd dealt with a hangover, but it was getting harder every year. He was almost thirty, and though most of the time the years passed without much changing, he felt it when it came to his alcohol tolerance.

Floyd rubbed himself dry, walking slowly back to his bedroom to pull on clean, comfortable clothes – old jeans and a t-shirt, and a light zip-up sweater.

When he was dressed, he made his cautious way to the kitchen for toast and orange juice, then gulped down pills. It took scrambled eggs and bacon before he felt semi-decent again, and he didn't bother cleaning up the dishes yet. He could do that when he got home.

He was already going to be a couple minutes late picking up his mother. More and he'd just get yelled at.

Floyd grabbed his sketchbook and pens on the way out the door. He walked as quickly as he dared to the car, shielding his eyes against the light, even though his body was fast shrugging off the effects of the extra beer or two last night. He wasn't entirely sure how many that had been, but there'd been a day he could slam a six-pack and not even feel it.

It was probably just as well he felt it now. That was probably how normal people reacted, not... people with issues like he'd once had.

As he pulled up in his parents' driveway, Floyd already saw his mother leaving the house, her handbag on her arm and her lips pursed tightly.

Oh, shit. I'm in for it.

"Good afternoon," she emphasized as she climbed into

the passenger seat, and Floyd glanced at the clock. Only eight minutes past noon.

"Sorry I'm late," Floyd said automatically, avoiding her gaze as he waited for her to buckle up, then pulled back down the driveway.

She eyed him critically, and he could just *feel* the comments itching at her tongue. *Might as well get them out,* he thought bitterly. Sure enough, moments later, she told him, "You don't look like you're ready to shop."

"I'm staying in the car. I have some work I have to get done."

"Hm."

Floyd adjusted his sun visor. "Where are you going to first?"

"The glasses place. I need to pick up my prescription."

"Right. Which one do you go to?" Floyd asked.

"The same one I used to take your brother to."

Aaand there it is. The guilt trip, all over again. It was the same tired guilt trip she used every damn time he did anything she didn't approve of. His little brother, dead for six years now, was still a weapon against him. And it was always "your brother" instead of his name – Ethan.

Ethan, a year younger than Floyd, had killed himself in college. In some fucked-up way, it was the first reason Floyd had signed up as a cop – so he could try to save others.

But that was old news now.

Floyd swallowed down his annoyance as always and straightened up in the driver's seat, not bothering to respond yet. He merged into traffic to drive them up toward the clinic.

"Your brother was always on time," his mother continued,

her lips twisting. "Always showed up a few minutes early, didn't he?"

"All right, I'm sorry," Floyd muttered, a bit sharper than he'd meant to. "I already said sorry."

"I just think it's inconsiderate to keep me waiting."

He didn't answer. *Don't take the bait.* "What time is your appointment?"

"I don't have one. I'm just picking my prescription up."

"Mm." *Damn. That would keep her out of the car for a while.* Floyd felt terrible thinking it, but some days, there was no talking to her.

And he couldn't complain. They still accepted him even after the couple years of uselessness. He'd mooched off them and felt sorry for himself after quitting the force and before opening the shop.

That was the other thing he tried not to think about too much. Between his brother's death and quitting his parents' dream job for him, he was something of a disappointment to his family. They didn't even know why things had ended with Brett – they'd liked him a lot.

He rubbed his face again, trying to will away the buzz of medication and frustration upsetting his stomach.

When she stepped out and walked into the clinic, he sat back and grabbed his sketchbook, letting a mental image of Greyson's arms come into his head.

Lots of canvas to work with. God, they were going to look good.

CHAPTER

Twelve

KEVIN

T**HE PHONE RANG SEVERAL TIMES, AND** K**EVIN FROWNED TO** himself as he rubbed his cheeks. He was waking up early considering it was the day after a game, but Floyd's last text had been cryptic. It had just said, *I hate mornings.*

He worried about Floyd more these days, since he'd left. They'd bonded quickly as soon as Chase had introduced them. While Floyd was easy enough to get along with, there was a lot more to him that he just didn't talk about.

Chase was probably his other closest friend, and he'd promised Kevin he'd keep an eye on him, but even so...

"Hello," he finally heard Floyd's scratchy morning voice answer.

"Hey," Kevin greeted. "It's me. How you doin'?"

"Oooof," Floyd groaned his complaint. "Out driving my mother around doing errands and shit. How'd the practice game go?"

"Not bad. This trainer is intense," Kevin laughed. "Cam's right about that. He caught... a few weaknesses, I guess... and sort of yelled them across the ice..." He imitated Glenn's voice. "Back-checking, Kevin! Fight for your space, Kevin!"

Floyd laughed. "Well, at least he doesn't bullshit you."

"He sure doesn't." Kevin rolled out of bed, rubbing his face. "What's up with this morning? Other than your mother?"

"Hangover," Floyd said simply.

Kevin winced. He knew Floyd had once had an issue with drinking – Floyd usually turned down beers after the third or fourth one, and he'd only once let that slip – but he didn't know why. "You went on a bender, eh?"

"Not intentionally. Just got carried away. Hanging out with the guys, and then someone else showed up."

"Who's that?" Kevin's interest was piqued.

"Some guy I once knew from the force."

"The..." *Oh yeah, he was a cop before.* Floyd had mentioned that once or twice, too. God, he was mysterious sometimes. "Right, no, never mind. As a cop?"

"Yeah."

"That must've been good." *Or maybe not,* Kevin thought, wincing. "Right?"

"Yeah, more or less." There was something off in Floyd's voice. "So, talk to me about camp, though."

"It's... I don't know how to describe it," Kevin laughed. "It's living and breathing the damn sport." His roommate, Hans, was a lot less charitable: he described it as hell on ice, then roller blades, then staircases...

But Kevin liked the challenge. New exercises, new routines, and Glenn never let them get old. He'd only been there a week and he'd already played practices in every position – with other guys and alone – just to help Glenn assess his skills. He'd done about eight types of sports, plus tried new gym exercises his old coach had never suggested.

It was a whole new league here.

"All the guys are great, though," he continued. "I've talked to them about Cam a bit and most of them knew him. Everyone mentioned Matty as his best friend," he laughed. "I only met the guy once, though, when they introduced us all to each other. Did they ever...?"

"What?" Floyd exclaimed with a laugh. "Cam and Matty?"

Kevin laughed. "I don't know, man. It seems pretty... gay here."

Floyd burst out laughing. "Really?"

"Really. I mean, loudly straight, but quietly gay..." He couldn't say a lot more with his roommate in the same apartment, maybe listening in, though. "Anyway, it's great here."

Kevin didn't want to admit he missed their chosen family of friends and boyfriends.

"How's it gonna go on the road?"

"Good, I hope," Kevin admitted. "Assuming I ever go. I keep screwing up like this..."

"You'll be fine," Floyd assured him, that deep voice oddly calming. He had that certain way of calming people, and Kevin wasn't even sure Floyd knew it. Maybe he did, though. It would be a useful skill for a tattoo artist.

"So what's your family up to now?"

"Mom's got me driving her all around town," Floyd lamented. "And, like I said, hangover... it's not so bad though. It's getting better now. I was a couple minutes late, though, so she started with passive-aggression..."

"Ohhh. Ouch," Kevin winced. From the tiny hints Floyd had dropped – again, subtly, because the man didn't seem to like to admit to his problems – it sounded like his parents were a little overbearing.

"It's cool though."

Kevin disagreed, but he kept that to himself. "Got your eye on anyone out there that I don't know about?"

Floyd groaned. "Kevin. Jesus, it's been like a week."

Kevin laughed. "So what? You can meet someone in a week. If you're like the Rileys, you can practically get engaged in a week..."

"Ohhh," Floyd laughed, but finally it was a hearty sound. "I'll tell them you said that."

"They can't deny it!" Kevin noticed that Floyd hadn't actually answered the question, where he usually would have given an exhausted, *No*, groan. Particularly given his worries about finding someone to come with him to the reunion...

"Mmm," Floyd said, cutting off his train of thought before he could form the question. "So what about you?"

Kevin hesitated, scratching at his head. It was still too early to say, but...

"I can't afford to fuck things up," Kevin told him. "So... no. I'm just keeping my head down. I don't know who's who yet."

"Of course." Floyd sounded sympathetic. "I know exactly what that's like."

From being a cop? Well, yeah, actually... now that he thought about it, that seemed like a similar environment. Kevin nodded to himself. "It gets easier though, huh?"

"Definitely. Okay, I gotta eat and hit the gym again."

"Okay. You take care, eh?" Floyd told him.

"You too, man." For all Kevin's worries, Floyd sounded all right. "Keep me in the loop."

"Will do. Bye."

Once he hung up, Kevin pulled his covers up to halfheartedly make his bed, then turned to ruffle his hair in the mirror and try to wake up.

I hope Floyd's okay out there with all those lovebirds. Kevin knew how easy it was to compare himself to everyone else around getting some and feel... lacking.

Floyd was a great guy, though. He'd find someone. Maybe, just maybe... he already had met the right guy. Floyd just had to convince *himself* of it.

CHAPTER
Thirteen

GREYSON

"So, you busy tonight?"

Greyson hadn't expected Alan to initiate conversation. After that weird exchange or two, he'd just written him off. Now, as he leaned against the desk to check the sign-in list for his class, Alan was talking to him?

He'd take it, though.

"Not very. Just one class, and then... working out by myself, at last." Greyson laughed. It was weird after working everyone else out, but he often didn't get the kind of burn he craved from it. He spent too much time teaching and correcting – not that he minded that.

"I meant after work."

Oh, shit. Greyson's eyebrows shot up and he paused, then shook his head. "No." *I'll let him ask me out, though...*

Alan casually turned to write his number on a scrap of paper and held it out. "You wanna meet me?"

That was ballsy. Greyson took the paper automatically and glanced at it, then paused. *What if people think I'm... exploiting my job somehow? Oh, fuck it.*

"Sure."

The thrill that ran through him wasn't entirely victorious. That was odd.

"See you soon." Alan winked.

Greyson's chest lurched with realization. *Ohhhh. Shit, no.* He couldn't believe it. One fucking kiss with Floyd last night – one hard kiss, yeah, but one nonetheless... and now he was ready to swear off other men? That was fucking stupid. He'd been eying Alan for weeks now.

Greyson reminded himself that he'd *wanted* this.

"See you," he answered with a grin, then strode casually to the back room. He kept the paper still clutched tightly in his fist. "Ohhh, fuck," he whispered once he got there at last, leaning against the locker and thumping his head.

That was stupid.

Greyson was going to enjoy himself, damn it.

"What's up?"

It was the second time in as many days someone snuck up on him, and Greyson's heart lurched again as he jolted. "Jesus."

"Sorry," Jake laughed, stepping out from the storage room with yoga mats under his arm. "Everything okay?"

"Fine, fine," Greyson assured him with a laugh. "Just tired. Out late last night. Gotta sweat out the beer."

Jake laughed. "I feel that," he agreed, reaching out for an awkward fist bump on the way by as he juggled the yoga mats under his arm.

Greyson chewed his lip, then opened his fist again once Jake was gone to program the number into his phone under *Alan.*

That night, Greyson texted Alan an hour or so after he left the gym. He took the time to eat supper, shower properly, and change into another long-sleeved light shirt and jeans. It was still only eight or so, hopefully early enough in the evening that it wasn't too weird. He sent a simple text.

Hey, it's Greyson.

Alan's response was instant.

Hi. Wanna come over?

Greyson licked his lips. Alan wasn't wasting any time.

Sure, what's your address?

Alan answered with it at almost the same moment, like he'd already been composing the message. Greyson stared at it until the address registered, then pocketed his phone and set out for the drive.

When he pulled up outside the well-lit little house, Greyson raised his eyebrows. Alan was here? On his own, or with someone? It looked like a small house, maybe two or three bedrooms at most... a starter home for a couple, or a good home for a single.

The outside was immaculate, though. Alan was *definitely* gay.

Greyson laughed under his breath, locking his car and walking up the path toward the front door. When he knocked, Alan was quick enough to answer.

It was strange seeing his coworker in his own house instead of behind the Y desk. The house was clean and bright, and there was no sign of anyone else around. "Hey," Greyson said.

Alan held the door open for him. "Hi. How's it going?"

"Good, good. Had a good day at work?"

"Fine," Alan shrugged. His eyes were already wandering

up and down Greyson's body as he pushed the door shut. His shirt was only halfway buttoned up, his feet bare.

Greyson decided to cut to the chase. "I'm not here for coffee, am I?"

Alan hesitated, then jerked his chin in a quick nod. "No."

"I knew it." Greyson smirked, stepping slowly closer to get into Alan's space. "You were playing hard-to-get, weren't you?"

Alan grinned. "I wanted to make you work for it," he retorted. "Come on in."

They walked together to the couch, but before Greyson could even sit down, Alan was pushing him onto his back along the length of it.

That was fine by him. Greyson's nerves sparked, and he hissed a quiet approval through his teeth as Alan rolled onto the couch, his face at crotch level.

Blowjobs? That's cool.

"You want me to...?" Alan murmured, his hand running up the inside of Greyson's thigh until Greyson shuddered with wanting.

"I do."

Alan crouched above Greyson as he pushed his shirt up, kissing his stomach and lapping at his abs. Greyson was used to guys being impressed by them, so he hauled up his shirt a little further and Alan cast an appreciative look up and down.

Then, Alan slid the button out of his jeans and pulled them down around Greyson's thighs, his fingers wrapping around his cock and pulling it out into open air.

The forthright attention had Greyson half-hard already with imagining – those pretty, full lips wrapped around his cock... Mmm.

Alan licked the head and whispered, "I love getting glimpses of this through your sweatpants. You oughta go commando more."

Greyson's eyebrows shot up, and then he grinned. He only did now and then, but apparently, Alan had been watching. "Yeah? Maybe I will," he teased.

Alan smirked, his lips closing around the tip as he sucked the hardening flesh into his mouth. Hot, wet warmth enveloped him and sank down to the base, and the ridges of his palate rubbed across the head.

"Mmm." Greyson rolled his head back, his hips arching a little until Alan pushed on his stomach to get him to stay flat. Alan's mouth worked around him, his tongue lapping under and around his cock as he sucked his cheeks in.

Floyd would look hotter sucking him off.

Ohhhh, shit. Nope. Don't even fucking go there! Greyson had a strict rule against thinking of one guy while he was with another.

Still, the image of Floyd's rippling muscles and dark, penetrating eyes and big, rough hands wouldn't leave his head.

Especially *those* beautiful, wet lips wrapping around his cock.

Greyson swallowed a moan and curled his fingers into the couch while Alan sucked him harder, bobbing his head in a quick, up-and-down rhythm not meant to prolong this.

Picturing Floyd's hands wandering over his body, touching him with the same firm, yet gentle grip as he'd used on Greyson's arm while evaluating him...

Or the firmness of his handshake...

How good would those fingers feel wrapped around his cock?

"Nnh-- almost--" Greyson started to warn Alan.

"Mmm." Alan pulled back a little but let Greyson's cock stay on his tongue as he sucked the head.

"Jesus!" When he came, Greyson squeezed his eyes shut, his body's tension finally coiling up once more, as tightly as possible, before his muscles spasmed and released. And all he could see was Floyd drinking down his passion, staring at him with the full intensity of his gaze.

"Oh, fuck," he whispered, trying to catch his breath as Alan's mouth slipped off his cock, his shudders subsiding as his body sank back to the couch.

Time to return the favor, and though it made him almost shift with guilt, he knew exactly what he was going to see when he made this offer. Not that Alan ought to care – he was getting the best side-effect of these thoughts.

"Get on up," Greyson patted his chest.

Alan's eyes widened, but he wasted no time crawling up until he straddled Greyson's shoulders, one knee just about slipping off the edge of the couch. He unzipped himself, pulling out his dick along the way.

It was hard already, which made Greyson grin. Alan liked giving head, then. Or he'd been fiddling with himself the whole time, which was the same difference.

What would Floyd look like, naked? Did he have tattoos up along his stomach and chest and shoulders? Would he be moaning already, quietly, like Alan was?

Alan was slender enough and easy to haul closer so he could suck that cock at just the right angle, swallowing the warm, firm length until it almost hit the back of his throat before bobbing his head back again. Even at this angle, he wasn't big enough to choke him, so Greyson was free to let his imagination wander.

He sucked eagerly, not easily able to see Alan's face from this angle and also not particularly caring. When Alan warned him he was close, he ignored it, though. Like Alan, he was gonna swallow.

Alan's cock swelled and then released in quick, sticky loads that hit the back of his throat as his whole body shuddered. He nearly lost his balance and Greyson grabbed his hip to keep him steady.

"Oh, fuck... yes!"

When Alan went still, Greyson pulled back a little, then let him scoot backward on his knees until he could zip up again.

"That was good," Alan breathed out.

"Oh, yeah." Greyson couldn't help but grin. *Not for the reasons you think, but... it was awesome.* Now he knew he was officially lusting after his ex-partner. He just had to figure out how to chase him.

The oddest part, though, was how cool Alan seemed to be now that the blowjobs were over. It wasn't like Greyson expected cuddles by the fireplace, but he was acting almost... snobby? He looked like he was waiting for Greyson to thank him.

Greyson's heart sank. Alan thought Greyson should be grateful for this.

Fuck that. Alan got just as much out of it as him.

"That was cool," Greyson concluded, zipping up as he stood up. "See you at work, a'ight?" he drawled, keeping it low-key.

Alan looked surprised, then a little miffed. "Yeah. Sure."

Greyson sauntered to the door. "See you." He didn't look back as he let himself out, striding down the sidewalk to the car.

For a moment, he almost felt bad. Maybe he'd misread that. Then, he reminded himself of his number one rule: *always trust your gut instinct.*

Greyson wasn't damaged goods, and he was never going to act like he was.

Just before he reached the house, a text message buzzed in his pocket, so Greyson dug out his phone. His eyebrows rose a few moments later.

Oh.

Hey, it's Floyd. I have preliminary sketches done, can you email me pics tonight of designs and styles you like?

Greyson's cheeks flushed. He waited until he was in the house to answer – until he kicked off his shoes and grabbed his laptop. Then, he responded.

Yeah sure! I'll email them tonight.

A few moments later, he got a response.

Awesome. Floyd sent his email address, which was the same as always.

It took him a little while on Google and different tattoo forums to collect photos that he liked – especially of the kinds of scenery he wanted. He really wanted one with the Rockies, since he'd grown exceptionally fond of the landscape out in Alberta. On the other arm, he could have Atlantic Canadian scenery.

And the angel wings... well, it was a stereotype, but in dotwork and greyscale it at least wouldn't look the same as every other goddamn angel wing tattoo out there. That would also leave him room to tattoo around in the blank spaces and get them filled in sometime, if he wanted to make them more like conventional sleeves.

He attached all the photos to his email, then addressed it to Floyd.

That was an email he hadn't used in years. His new email account didn't even recognize it.

It was a hard decision on what to type in his message, but Greyson finally settled on:

Here are some photos. Thanks, man. It was good to see you yesterday.

He pressed send, a shiver of anxiety crawling down his spine. He tried to brush it off, instead grabbing the TV remote while he kept the laptop open all evening. Just in case.

By the time Greyson went to bed, he hadn't gotten a response.

At least we're probably still on for Friday, he thought as he shut everything down for the night. At least, he hoped he hadn't screwed anything up by hinting at that moment between them.

That moment he'd so loved.

CHAPTER
Fourteen

FLOYD

A BADGE ON HIS GRINDR ICON ALERTED FLOYD TO ANOTHER new message. He just hoped it wasn't some twink pissed off at him for ignoring his messages.

Luckily, it wasn't... but a moment after reading it, Floyd realized he would have preferred that.

It was a message from the blank profile he'd spotted earlier.

And worse yet, it said, *I think you know me.*

"Fuck," Floyd whispered. It wasn't the first time he'd gotten that message – the community was damn small enough, after all – but it was the first time from a faceless profile. That made it a lot creepier.

He rubbed his chin, looking at the guy's profile again before going back to the message. It seemed like the opening to a horror movie if he didn't answer.

Were we in school together? he guessed. Half the awkward Grindr interactions he'd ever had in this city were from former schoolmates. The answer was almost immediate.

Yeah lol.

Floyd narrowed his eyes suspiciously.

Ok then who are you?

There was no answer just yet, and not for a few minutes.

Floyd tried not to let his imagination run away with him as he leaned back, not even bothering looking at the other guys nearby. He just left that message chain open until another message came through.

I'll see you at the reunion soon anyway lol you single?

Floyd raised his eyebrows. It was on his damn profile that he was, but why was this guy worried about it? Was he looking for someone to go with, too? That could be a convenient excuse, if he knew who the guy was.

Who was gay in his year that he didn't already know about? He rubbed his chin, trying to cast his mind back through soccer players, hockey stars, quiet nerds, emos, punks...

It could be anyone.

Yeah, Floyd answered simply.

Then, his heart sank as the obvious occurred to him. It could be Brett.

The asshole had tried to message on Facebook a couple months ago and had talked about the reunion then, too.

Floyd had called Alex, the private detective, for help making sure Brett wasn't stalking him. But before going through with it, he'd backed out to deal with it himself.

He didn't want anyone knowing about that.

But now... if he was back...

This would make a hell of a lot of sense, given that the other guy didn't seem to want to show his face or name.

Did we date? Floyd asked next, staring at the Grindr message chain. He waited for longer than he had for the last message and still nothing came through.

He flicked back to Brett's Facebook message on his laptop, taking a minute to find the conversation. He'd blocked the guy after getting the message, but he still had it around, just in case.

Hey man how are you. Coming into Freddy for the reunion we should meet up lol.

That was all he'd said, but that was enough to raise Floyd's hackles. The little asshole, thinking he wanted him around again after all that had happened.

But Floyd was older now. He could look after himself, and he wasn't so blinded by Brett's supposed love for him. He wasn't that weak anymore.

Floyd's phone went off and he checked the conversation. His stomach lurched at the response.

ya.

He put down his phone for a minute, trying to come up with some response that was more eloquent than just *fuck off*. "No, that's enough," he muttered under his breath a moment later and went back to his profile.

It was gone.

"What the--"

Brett had deleted his fucking profile. Of course he had.

"What a fuckin' creepy skeevy asshole," Floyd muttered under his breath. Then again, Brett always had been. Alex couldn't help him if the guy just wanted to creep him out anyway.

Then there was the irony of reconnecting with both Greyson and Brett at the same time. And what a cruel fuckin' irony *that* was.

But Floyd was pissed this time. He'd had years to get ready for this. He wasn't going to let *anyone* tell him who or what to do.

CHAPTER
Fifteen
GREYSON

"OKAY, GOOD ENOUGH." AS GREYSON STUDIED HIMSELF IN THE bathroom mirror, he let his chest push forward. He stood in the attention-grabbing pose of a guy who knew exactly how to handle the situation, even if he didn't.

He looked *more* than good enough.

But he was in a short-sleeved shirt, the arms stretching tight around his biceps. It showed off his forearms, which he knew was a good thing in general, but also his inner arms.

What a bizarre contrast that was. He was tired of being self-conscious, even if he'd been dealing with it for years. Realistically, it wasn't like *everyone* noticed, his muscles and hair doing enough to hide the marks many times, but sometimes it felt like they would.

Greyson shoved his phone and wallet into his pockets, then checked for his keys before striding out of the house. He decided to walk instead of taking the car, needing the exercise to cool his nerves.

This was his first time seeing Floyd since that drunken kiss, and he just prayed Floyd didn't have to be wasted again to look him in the eye. If he'd fucked something up between them, he was going to regret it.

When he approached the shop a minute or two before he was due, he slowed his pace to walk the last few blocks so he'd get there right on time.

The door jangled as he pushed it open.

"Hey," Floyd greeted immediately from behind the counter, ducking out from behind it to approach him. "You made it."

Greyson half-expected a hug or a handshake or something, but Floyd stepped around him to flip the sign to "closed" and turn the lock on the door.

"Oh... Hey. You're – am I on time...?"

Floyd laughed. "Yeah. I just can't take on any new customers if I'm working on you, and I'd rather not. I often close for my evening appointment."

"Oh." Greyson felt a bit sheepish for what he'd been starting to think. He cleared his throat, then wandered up to the counter.

Floyd cut him a sideways glance. "Ready to go over everything? Come through to the back."

That night hadn't been the end of their chemistry, then. As Floyd brushed past him, bare arms touched, and he saw Floyd straighten up a little at the same moment as a shiver rushed down Greyson's spine.

He followed into the back room again. "No Chase?"

"Nah, I close the shop today."

"Cool." Greyson sprawled on the chair, knees apart, trying to sit sideways while Floyd pushed his chrome-legged rolling stool closer and sat on it, opening up his book.

"Oh, wow."

The designs were *gorgeous*. The intricate dots laced

around each other, forming individual feathers from the elbow out. The feathers were grouped along his arm in a way that looked just like wings. The best part, though, was the sketch of mountain scenery. A crisp lake sat in a pool at the bottom of the mountain, with one tree branch cutting across the field of vision just like a photograph. And it looked like that could go over the deepest scar.

"That's..." Greyson looked over at the other arm. The design was quite similar, only the feathers were thicker and more tufty, looking almost three-dimensional. He actually touched them just to make sure they weren't, and Floyd laughed. "I wanted to check!"

"You like that one more?"

"I... think I prefer the first one."

"Mmm." Floyd nodded, obviously making a mental note of that. "And that scenery?"

It was a rocky cliff, but unmistakably Atlantic Canadian: short, stout trees and a lighthouse in the background.

"Beautiful," Greyson approved, looking up at Floyd.

Oh, shit, he was close. They weren't even a foot apart, and Floyd's eyes were fixed on his expressions.

"Thanks," Floyd said, his voice quiet. "I was hoping you'd like them. You can be honest, though, if there's anything you want me to change."

"No." Greyson really meant it. He hadn't expected the art to come *that* quickly, or to be that... well... artistic. Floyd was incredible.

He just couldn't imagine it on his own skin.

"So," Floyd abruptly said, uncapping his pen, "what was up with that kiss?"

Greyson's jaw dropped, and then he laughed under his breath. "You started it."

"No, you did."

"We both probably did," Greyson snorted as Floyd started to grin. "'cause we were both... pretty into it."

Floyd shared a laugh with him, then rolled closer. "Lie down on the chair."

Greyson shifted and stretched out his legs, then laid his arm along the armrest. "Like this?"

"Perfect." Floyd's hand touched his arm, turning it this way and that as he examined his sketchbook. He spoke with a flatter tone to his voice, as if most of his concentration was going into the art, but his eyes were alert when they flicked up to Greyson's. "Didn't know you were gay back then. Why'd you come out now?"

"I didn't know 'til Alberta," Greyson murmured, keeping his voice down even though nobody else was around the shop. All his anxiety about meeting up with Floyd again, about what he might say or about the tension that might be between them... It was all gone. He relaxed under Floyd's touch and his deep, steady voice. "So I'm not exactly closeted here. I just haven't told people yet."

"Mmm. So, what do you think about the lake across these ones, with this tree branch – and those cliffs across here?"

"That was what I figured you'd do. It looked great on the paper."

"Hold still." Floyd flipped his arm over until the back of his hand pressed the arm rest, rolling closer and sketching in quick, certain motions with his fine-tipped pen. Line by line, he outlined the art with breathtaking precision.

Though Greyson's stomach naturally knotted when the pen went across his scars, it didn't seem to stop it. "Will the ink hold differently...?"

"It sometimes does. I've tattooed over worse and they do

bleed a little, but you can touch up areas," Floyd told him. "It's free. Speaking of which..."

Greyson laughed quietly. "I know it's gonna be expensive. I looked up your rate."

"Perfect," Floyd nodded. "I'm thinking about twenty hours per arm."

"Okay." Greyson had been expecting a little longer, actually. "You must be fast."

"This is my preferred style." Bit by bit, the landscape flowed up Greyson's arm, and he was fascinated by the progression of black ink. "I'm slower at other styles. That's why we always have complementary artists at the shop."

"Mmm. I'm lucky I like your style, then," Greyson said. He shivered at each brush of Floyd's fingers along his arm, even if they were strictly professional.

Floyd's eyes flickered to him for a moment before he smiled. "I'm glad, too. How does that look?"

"That's perfect."

"Now I'll do the angel wings. More like this than that, yeah?"

"Yeah. Maybe with a couple more feathers..."

Floyd watched attentively as he pointed out the changes he wanted made, and he was quick to translate them to Greyson's skin. The marker almost tickled as he drew along the inner arm.

"I'll have to shave your arms first, before I can do the upper parts, though." Floyd was already rolling away to grab a razor.

"No problem," Greyson told him. "Now?"

"Yep. By the way – does tomorrow morning still work for you to start the tattooing? It's going to take a while to get all these details worked out. The ink lasts a couple days if we need to book next week."

"Yeah, that's perfect. Oh, how about something a little higher – yeah, right there," Greyson smiled as Floyd's pen worked across his skin. "Jesus, you're fast."

"I've done it for a while," Floyd dryly responded with a grin. "You're still fast with handcuffs, I bet."

"Right. Sorry," Greyson laughed. That *hadn't* been meant as innuendo, he was sure. Had it...?

They chatted lightly over the next few minutes as Greyson turned his arm this way and that to let Floyd shave off the hairs of his arms. Floyd's touch was firm, and the feeling of the razor sliding smoothly across his skin made him catch his breath with how surprisingly erotic it was.

It was so much trust to place in him, but he didn't doubt Floyd for a second.

Once his arms were smooth enough, Floyd resumed drawing, his marker working quickly.

Still, the last half-hour had done nothing to dispel Greyson's yearning for Floyd's touch, and it was only getting harder to restrain his impulses. Being close to Floyd for long enough to talk to him was bad enough, but minutes upon minutes of Floyd turning his arms around, holding them down, drawing on him, the grazes of fingers along his skin...

It was all he could do not to get hard.

Finally, Floyd murmured, "Check that out. I'll get you a mirror."

Greyson was stunned at even the line art on his skin. It was like nothing he'd ever seen. He couldn't have pictured it before he saw it, but now that he had, it just looked *good* on him. "Wow."

"You'll carry them very well," Floyd nodded. "You have the right build for this style of sleeve."

"Guess so," Greyson grinned, turning his arms this way and that to see himself with the line art. "Yeah, that's – all of that is what I want."

"No changes?"

"None," Greyson told him, finally tearing his eyes off the mirror as Floyd set it aside and sat down again. "So, tomorrow morning we start the line art?"

Floyd nodded, peeling off his gloves and throwing out the marker. "And you'll want to wash your sheets tonight to promote better healing."

Greyson slowly sat up. "Okay. Better get laid tonight, then."

Floyd, who had been tensing up to roll away, froze and gazed at him levelly. Greyson saw the heat flush through his cheeks in a red wave, and then Floyd's lips parted to say something.

Greyson swung his legs over the edge of the chair until their legs touched.

Floyd's eyes darkened, and he wordlessly leaned in.

Greyson grabbed him by the cheeks to haul him closer and they were kissing, both rising to their feet and stumbling against each other as they kissed hard. Those warm hands which had so patiently worked over his skin for minutes on end now clutched at his shoulders and grabbed the front of his shirt, hauling him even closer.

Floyd was solid and warm against his front, his lips soft but his cock hard. It pressed against Greyson even through layers of denim, and Greyson *burned* to feel it without anything in the way.

Hands already ran up bodies, each of them taking a

moment to feel up each other's builds. God, Floyd was even fitter now than he had been back then – his biceps properly filled out, his chest a solid mass of muscle, his stomach tight and rippling...

But was that strength all outward, or was it core?

Fucking was a great way to find out.

Greyson hungrily pushed against Floyd, grinding into his hip as they gasped for breath into each other's mouths, already half-tearing each other's shirts off.

"Wait," Floyd whispered, which made Greyson's heart lurch. But Floyd sure as hell wasn't pushing him back – his hands were on Greyson's hips, pulling him close. "Come home with me. If we're gonna do this, it's at my place, not here."

Greyson jerkily nodded. "All right."

"Just think of the sanitization."

That startled a laugh out of Greyson, and then he was laughing louder than he had, in longer than he could remember, stumbling against Floyd before he straightened up.

He was grinning freely, too, his eyes lighting up with joy. Going home with this man? Oh, *fuck*, yes.

"I'll be out in three minutes. I just have to clean up in here and set the alarm. Don't fuckin' go anywhere," Floyd warned as Greyson pulled away for the door.

"Aye aye, sir," Greyson winked. He fumbled with the handle until he got out into the hall, then made his way through the front and waited on the sidewalk outside.

Greyson's heart still pounded with the memory of that hot, hard body pressing against his, claiming every bit of pleasure that he could give. And soon, he was going to have a lot more to remember than that.

His arms were inked up, his cock was on fire, and his

mind was blown. Never in a thousand years had he imagined they would *actually* fuck, but this man was taking him home.

For the first time in a long time, as he waited on the sidewalk, Greyson couldn't *wait* for his partner for tonight to join him.

Sixteen

FLOYD

GREYSON LOOKED HOT LOUNGING OUTSIDE THE SHOP WAITING for him to lock up, hot leaning against the car door waiting to be let in, and hot sprawled back in his passenger seat.

Floyd was just fucking *into* him, no matter what.

Then there were Greyson's beautiful eyes. They so seriously met his whenever Greyson talked about what he'd gone through. He used blunt, quick words that definitely didn't cover the extent of what he'd seen and done in the last few years. Those eyes had been fixed on him for that entire art session, watching him so hard Floyd's dick had started to hurt.

Was it any wonder he could hardly control himself around the man?

There was something about his smile, and the way he watched him, and even the way he spoke – full of authority, but tentative under that. Some part of him was... always asking for permission, like he knew what he was doing at work but he was totally out in left field here.

It wasn't like Greyson *actually* didn't know what he was

doing. Not with the way he kissed. Floyd wondered if those scars ran deeper than they seemed. Maybe he didn't think of himself anywhere *near* as hot as he came off.

They almost fell into Floyd's apartment, already kissing before they closed the door.

"Jesus," Greyson whispered, his voice hoarse and a little strung out as he grabbed Floyd's shoulders to keep himself from tripping.

Floyd grinned, guiding him through the entryway. He kicked his shoes off and waited for Greyson to do the same, then pulled him close with one quick yank to grind together again.

"Which way's your room?"

"That way." Floyd grabbed Greyson's ass, then laughed at his expression of surprised arousal and pulled him along toward it.

Greyson pushed the door shut after them both, then grabbed Floyd's cheeks to pull him in again for a long, filthy kiss. They pressed each other up against the bedroom door and Floyd let Greyson flatten him against it to give a few quick, suggestive thrusts of their hips together and let their cocks get hard again.

He was about ready to fuckin' come in his pants, but there was no *way* could he let himself do that.

Not until he'd had a taste of Greyson in all his ripped glory.

They wasted no time pulling each other's shirts off, biting at ears and necks and kissing at their lips between garments. When they were both shirtless, Floyd pulled Greyson in again so their nipples lightly brushed, circling his hips in slow, certain grinding moves as he pressed gentle, teasing open-mouthed kisses against the side of his neck.

"Oh, fuck," Greyson moaned. "You'd better not be a tease."

"I'm not," Floyd breathed out, cocky despite being pinned against the door. "Cause I follow through."

Greyson pulled Floyd over to the bed, giving them both a chance to look at each other as they crashed onto the bed together.

"You're fuckin' ripped now," Floyd whispered, his eyes wandering around those inked-up biceps and forearms, then down his chest and stomach. He made himself drag his gaze back up to his face.

Greyson gave an arrogant little grin and wink. "I know."

Floyd snorted with laughter, rolling Greyson onto his back and straddling him. He started attacking Greyson's chest and neck with kisses to melt that attitude. "Cheeky little fucker."

Greyson easily yielded, moaning and pushing up into Floyd's lips with each sucking kiss or nip against bare skin. His skin was soft and hot and tasted just like Floyd had imagined: musk and salt and... that unmistakable smell of *him*.

Floyd hadn't realized he'd missed Greyson's scent.

He licked up along Greyson's collarbone, then to the side of his neck. "Better not leave any marks if you're getting done tomorrow."

"Guess not," Greyson agreed, smirking. "What a shame."

Floyd nipped instead, a little sharper.

"Hnnh!" Greyson's nails bit into Floyd's shoulder, then scraped down his back as he hauled him up the bed to kiss his lips again.

Just *this* was intense – lips on lips, with soft, panting breaths against each other's mouths. They kept their eyes half-closed as if each was afraid to look the other straight in the eye.

This was going to be the hottest sex he'd had in *years*.

"Don't be freaked out if you see scars, yeah?"

Floyd snorted. "Course not," he assured Greyson with a shrug. "Don't be freaked out by my tats."

"Yeah," Greyson laughed. "What, you got one on your ass?"

"Smart-ass." Floyd smirked.

"It is a smart-ass. You got one?"

Greyson wrestled him a little, grabbing his biceps and heaving his body up against his to roll them over and pin Floyd down to the bed. Floyd gasped but let him, his adrenaline rushing at the sudden twist. Cool sheets made him shiver, but so did the hot mouth pressing a line down from the side of his neck to his nipple.

Floyd bit back his whimper of pleasure at the slow, dragging tease of a tongue around his nipple. Greyson knew how to use his mouth, then, the fucking sexy man. Floyd had to bite his lip hard to keep the sounds back, and even then, scattered ones slipped out.

"Hnn-nnh..." He squirmed, then raised a hand to his mouth to bite the side of his hand.

"Let me hear it," Greyson ordered hoarsely, his breath hot against the throbbing skin.

With great reluctance, Floyd let his hand fall away and tucked it behind his own head instead, then cried out at the first slow swipe of a tongue across the aching flesh.

The nub of skin seemed to connect straight to his cock, which was pulsing and throbbing with need in his pants. It was trapped and desperate for touch – or better yet, those gorgeous lips. Fuck, it almost hurt!

Floyd bit back another moan, then dug his nails into his palm hard when lips closed around his nipple and Greyson finally sucked it into his mouth.

"Oh, fuck. Fuck," he panted, his cheeks flushing with heat. Greyson had already found his weak spots, and they hadn't been on the bed more than three minutes.

Greyson chuckled deeply, apparently amused by his own discovery as he slowly let it pop out of his mouth, then sucked a few more times before kissing his way so slowly to the other nipple.

"I swear to God--" Floyd panted, gritting his teeth to resist the urge to haul Greyson's head over to the other nipple.

"Patience," Greyson teased, which *nearly* snapped Floyd's nerves. But he relented, his tongue swiping across the other nipple in rapid little flicks before he sucked that into his mouth, too.

Again, Floyd's cock throbbed, his other nipple still aching for more attention, too.

"I'll show *you* patience," Floyd whispered. "Hah!" Greyson had sucked it hard, making his head roll back and his spine arch off the bed again.

When he flopped down again, the last tingles from that intense burst of pleasure diffusing through his body, he was out of patience. He wrestled Greyson right back over again, grabbing his head to pin him to the pillow and kiss him hard – once, twice, three times...

Greyson gasped into his mouth, clutching him by the ass and grinding against him as he kissed back with teeth and tongue.

Floyd didn't let him have this pleasure for long. He wanted to tease every bit of a reaction out of Greyson in return. He yanked himself down and away, kissing along his neck to his ear, then behind it. A tongue along the lobe proved that Greyson's ears were sensitive, his skin twitching in a beautiful series of light ripples.

He flicked his tongue a few times, then dragged it all the way down to Greyson's collarbone.

"You're no better," Greyson grumbled.

Floyd smirked. "Patience," he mocked, kissing right above Greyson's nipple. "Good things come to those who-- nnh!" Greyson pushed his head down a little more to make him kiss his nipple. He burst out laughing, and so did Greyson. The laughter rippled through them both in an outbreak of pure joy, bizarrely out of place and yet perfect in that moment.

Then, he slapped Greyson's hand away, still laughing as he kissed the nipple properly a few times and flicked it with his tongue until he could suck it.

He kept on going, though, kissing down along his stomach as he pulled open Greyson's jeans to get him naked. On his chest and thighs, he found a few more scars – some looking like his wrists, others not self-inflicted at all. Wherever he found one, he kissed it.

"I'm gonna suck your cock," he breathed out, looking up Greyson's body.

Greyson's cheeks were flushed a beautiful red, and he didn't seem to know how to answer. He was still looking stunned. "Uh huh."

Floyd cracked a grin. "Finally, you're speechless."

"Shut up."

"Ah, well. Almost," Floyd mournfully shrugged, yanking his underwear and jeans down as he scooted down the bed.

Greyson's cock sprang free, straight and flushed red,

already clearly desperate for attention. Floyd was more than happy to give it to him once he'd fought the last of the clothes off Greyson's ankles.

First, though, he unbuttoned his own jeans and pulled them down enough to get his own cock out into the open. At least he could grind against Greyson a little.

"Hot," Greyson whispered, reaching down to stroke himself a few times as he looked Floyd up and down properly.

Floyd flushed with embarrassed pride, knowing Greyson's eyes were lingering on his tattoos. He paused long enough to give him a good view of them, then scooted back up the bed to replace Greyson's hand with his own around the base of the shaft.

Then, he kissed up the length to the very tip, kissed that, and let his lips smoothly part and slide around it and down.

"Hnnnh." Greyson's eyes slid closed as he rolled his head back. "Yeah...!"

Floyd loved seeing him in speechless pleasure, as much as he teased. He'd imagined his old partner now and then, in moments of guilty pleasure – once in the department men's bathroom, in a *really* desperate moment on a long shift.

But in person, hot and solid and writhing under him with need?

Fucking *incredible*.

He only got to suck that thick, swollen manhood into his mouth a few more times before Greyson gasped and pushed his head. "Don't – I wanna fuck you."

Floyd was flexible. For Greyson, he was *very* flexible. "Fuck, yeah," he whispered once he pulled his mouth off that wet, throbbing cock, looking up the length of Greyson's bare, tattooless skin. So much canvas he itched to work on.

"Get your ass up here."

Floyd grinned and scooted up the bed, then very deliberately rolled onto his front, burying his face in the pillow.

Just as he'd thought, Greyson couldn't resist. He was already on top of him, his weight blanketing Floyd from behind as he fumbled with his jeans to pull them down around his thighs.

"Oh, Christ, you're the hottest..." Greyson trailed off, seemingly wordless again. Was Floyd's blowjob game really *that* good?

Floyd grinned. "Thanks," he mumbled into the pillow, twisting so he could see behind him. Greyson was looking around, clearly in search of lubricant. Floyd spared him and leaned over to grab it for him.

Then, Greyson rummaged in his pocket and his wallet until he found a condom and tossed his jeans aside again, his dark eyes raking up and down Floyd's body. He grabbed the lubricant before Floyd could, and Floyd gasped.

"I want to do that."

Floyd's cheeks burned, but he nodded. Moments later, slick fingers pressed at his entrance and he moaned, pressing slowly up into them. "Y-Yes...!"

Greyson's fingers were thin and strong; rough, but not sharp. His touch was as careful as it was firm, and Floyd's resistance melted under the firm pressure.

Holy shit, this was a whole new tease.

The fingers in him were too thin compared to what he *really* wanted to be filled with, but he could barely moan his protest with how well they moved in him. In fact, Greyson was deliberately rubbing--

"Oh!" Floyd moaned, bucking up against Greyson's other hand on his lower back. "Oh, *fuck*." He'd found his prostate, and he was rubbing it like he wanted Floyd to come right now. "Christ, not that soon...!"

Greyson chuckled deeply. "I didn't know you were already on-edge." He lightened his touch, still rubbing for a minute more until Floyd's head spun.

"Please."

"Oh, yeah," Greyson whispered, pulling his fingers out.

Floyd pressed his face into his arm for a few moments to try to regain his composure, his whole world still spinning. How the fuck did Greyson get so good at fingering him? More importantly, was he going to be even better fucking him?

He had mere seconds before he found out.

The condom packet wrinkled from near his hip, and then Greyson's thick tip was pressing against his opening. Greyson tugged his jeans a little further down to make sure he had all the room he needed. The tight restriction of the fabric around Floyd's thighs kept his legs together, making it an even tighter squeeze.

Floyd was being filled suddenly, all warmth and hardness sliding into him as he curled his hands hard into the bedspread. Greyson's weight blanketed him, his solid muscles keeping him pressed in place, and the feeling of hot skin on skin was divine.

Christ, he loved being fucked.

Floyd dug his knees into the bed and pressed his fingertips into the bedspread, then bit the pillow. "Hnnh!"

Greyson's cock was filling him from top to bottom, the hot hardness making his mind spin. His already-hard cock throbbed with added pleasure of a type nothing else could imitate.

"That's it," Greyson roughly whispered into his ear, and

then lips were pressing behind his ear, a tongue lapping at that sensitive spot...

Floyd whimpered sharply when Greyson found the spot where all the nerves seemed to converge, making his body pulse with added pleasure and heat. The sheets were trapping his body heat beneath him, his body burning with fiery passion already.

Greyson rode him hard, plunging deep into him with each firm thrust of his hips. Floyd felt Greyson's thigh muscles ripple against his, and even the hitching breaths of his heaving chest. For his part, Floyd couldn't even get a hand under himself, but his cock was grinding against the silken sheets with almost enough pressure to get him off with that alone...

But that wasn't all. The head of that cock plunged past his prostate over and over, squeezing his pleasure out of him and sending hard jolts of need through his whole body.

"Yes!" Floyd moaned into the blankets, and Greyson's teeth closed around the back of his neck to nip for a moment before he kissed to the other side of his ear and licked along the rim.

The teasing-light, sensitive brushes of wet tongue against his skin made a sharp contrast to the fast, deep, endlessly satisfying pace Greyson set to fuck him, their hips driving together in sharp, pleasure-filled slaps.

"Yes, *please*... oh, God, yes," Floyd moaned, his mind spinning. He could almost forget that it was Greyson, his former partner, maybe one-time enemy, long-time friend...

Except that Greyson's scent was all around him, that distinct musk alongside the sharp smell of sex and sweat. Greyson's mouth was unmistakable in the way it moved across his skin, leaving twitching, tingling nerves in its wake.

Greyson's eyes bored into him from behind. Whenever Greyson took a pause from kissing him and pulled back even a little, Floyd only had to turn his head to the side to see the sharp way Greyson watched him.

"Yes...!"

That was Greyson, his voice a rough growl that sent chills of need through Floyd. The deep tone made Floyd's breath catch in his throat.

"Oh, *fucking hell*, Floyd, you're so much better... than I ever-- ah...!"

Whatever Greyson had been about to say, it was cut off by the short, sharp cry of a man in utter ecstasy. Floyd twisted his head around enough to watch Greyson's expression tauten and squeeze with pleasure as his mouth opened to gasp for breath.

That huge, swollen cock pounded him deeply a few more times with the sharp, jerky, desperate movements of Greyson's hips. Then, Greyson pulled out and back, his weight lifting off Floyd.

Already, Floyd missed being pinned to the bed by him, and he missed the cock in him.

But Greyson didn't make him wait for long, rolling him onto his back and scooting further down the bed to kiss along his stomach and thigh.

"Jesus!" Floyd yelped at how damn *sensitive* he was. His cock had been going entirely without attention for way too long now, and he was about ready to come at a single kiss.

"Hnnh-- nnh, yes..." Floyd panted, quickly tangling his hands in Greyson's hair. "Yes, please... fuck, yes..." He almost thrust into Greyson's mouth, but Greyson's hand on his hip kept him firmly pinned to the bed still.

The wet, tight warmth of suction around the tip of his

cock slid further down and Floyd groaned utterly senselessly with half-formed words of pleasure and approval and *need*.

Greyson sucked him off as the sparks of desire burst under his skin, and then everything narrowed to his focus on those beautiful, wide lips around his cock, the eager eyes on his own, and the wet warmth of that skilled tongue swiping around and along his frenulum.

"Yes...!" Floyd went off almost like a shot with no warning even for himself, his gasp at once horrified and apologetic, yet utterly thrilled. He tried to push Greyson back in the scarce seconds of warning he had, but Greyson wouldn't let him.

"Mmm," Greyson moaned encouragement instead, tightening his suction around the head as Floyd's passion spilled forth in hard, fast jolts of pleasure.

"G-Greyson, *yes*," was all Floyd could manage in a mumbled moan, his whole body convulsing with pleasure as his stomach tightened and his arms and legs twitched, and above all, the heat in his body still burned.

*Greyson is the hottest man I've ever, **ever** fucked.*

Even when Greyson pulled back from his softened cock, Floyd felt himself come down slowly as if he were still half on clouds. He could barely put three words together, his lips parted as he stared at Greyson.

"Well, you're easy to tucker out," Greyson murmured at last, grinning as he scooted back up to flop on his side next to Floyd.

Floyd rolled his eyes and turned onto his side to face Greyson. Once he kicked his jeans off to get naked, he reached out tentatively to rest his hand on Greyson's hip. That seemed like a safe bet. "J-Just takes me a minute, is all. After a great orgasm." And Christ, that *had* been.

"I'll accept that compliment," Greyson murmured, reaching around for a cheeky slap on Floyd's ass.

"Hey," Floyd laughed, his wits slowly recovering. Greyson *was* the hottest man he'd ever been with, but he had no idea if this was some stupid one-time thing or not. Maybe Greyson had just been unable to resist temptation, like him. Maybe he had... other plans.

Floyd hoped not.

"You can stay overnight," Floyd murmured, wiping his forehead and shifting where he lay so his limbs were more comfortable. He didn't care if he had to wash the bedding tomorrow morning.

"Nah," Greyson murmured, a pink flush rising up his cheeks. He was pretty hard to embarrass, but somehow, Floyd had managed it. He didn't quite know how. "I'll see you in the morning anyway, pretty early on. First, I have a couple things to do. Laundry, for one."

"Right. Your sheets." The thought of doing laundry at the same time as Greyson in another household made Floyd smile to himself. "Good man. Follow the care instructions."

"I will," Greyson agreed. There was a moment where they lay next to each other still, hands on each other's hips, eyes on each other, lips still parted as they caught their breath.

Then Greyson rolled up and away, pushing himself to his feet while Floyd closed his eyes to let him clean up and dress.

Floyd tried to get up to see him out, but Greyson shook his head. "I'll see myself out, it's all right."

Privately, Floyd was relieved to skip the weird moment that always happened at the door. He pushed himself up onto his elbow instead and nodded casually. "Cool."

"Yeah... cool." Greyson, now dressed and pulling his belt

through the last loop, paused and gazed at him, then nodded sharply. "See you tomorrow, still, yeah?"

Floyd nodded. *For hours. God, I shouldn't have started mixing business and pleasure.* But whatever. Floyd was too pleasantly exhausted to think about tomorrow yet.

He listened to Greyson leave the apartment and listened to the door click shut, then closed his eyes once he was sure it was secure.

Floyd wasted no time scrambling under the sheets, still remembering the weight of Greyson along his back and the thick, hot weight of Greyson inside him. If Floyd could've gotten hard again at the memory, he no doubt would have.

But just as much as the raw sensual details, he remembered the gentle touch of fingers along his spine and ribs, the gentle brush of lips against his ear...

Floyd was asleep within minutes.

CHAPTER
Seventeen

GREYSON

G RAVEL CRUNCHED UNDERFOOT, SQUEAKING AGAINST Greyson's shoes as he trotted down the lane toward the main road. The sun was barely up, even considering the summer hour, but anxious energy burned through Greyson and fueled him on.

He'd barely slept, but that was normal these days. Whether he slept for three hours or nine, he always woke with the crawling anxiety under his skin that *needed* release, and the healthiest way he knew to burn it off was by running.

So that morning, as most mornings, Greyson was out for a run. Unlike most of his class days, he pushed himself until his lungs burned. He didn't care if he had to fuel up extra to make up for it – he needed the burn of *doing* something that would keep him completely busy.

"Shit!" The word spilled from his lips as he backpedaled to a halt, his arms flailing. *He* had right of way at the cross-walk, but that didn't matter when some punk-ass kid in a Jeep didn't feel like stopping.

Greyson barely restrained the urge to flip the kid the middle finger as he roared through the crosswalk, but even more terrifying was the fact that the guy's eyes didn't even flicker his way. He hadn't even seen him.

"Asshole drivers in this asshole town," Greyson exclaimed, his voice breathless and grating even to his own ears as he ran across the crosswalk to finish the last, and paved, loop of his run. Then he'd turn around to trace his steps back home.

At least he'd seen the guy in time. His adrenaline still pumped hard, his body utterly consumed by that feeling of being *alive*, miraculously.

It wasn't like he'd been grazed on the way by. There were still a few feet of room to spare – a little distance. Greyson knew he wouldn't have made it across the crosswalk in time, though, and that was terrifying.

Greyson made it home fine, though his heart still pumped even harder than it ought to have by the end of the run. His legs had that great burning, trembling, itching feeling that always meant he'd just had the exact right length of run – not so long it hurt, but long enough to stretch him to his limits.

And as always, the first blast of hot shower water across the back of his neck was better than some orgasms.

Not the one last night, though.

Fuck, he still caught his breath even thinking about being pressed over and against Floyd's hot body, pounding him into the bed with single minded focus on making Floyd cry out his pleasure.

And had he ever. Floyd was noisy and squirmy in bed, perhaps kept a little more restrained by being half-dressed throughout their time in bed yesterday. Greyson really wanted him naked next time.

But more than that, he wanted to look into his eyes. Those brief glimpses of pleasure hadn't been enough for him. He wanted to see Floyd's ecstasy and joy and every moment of pleasure drawn across his face like a map.

Floyd was so damn easy to read. It was like he'd never been trained a day in the force, which... seemed like exactly what Floyd wanted, if he was so determined to ditch his old life. Not that Greyson could blame him for that.

"God," Greyson mumbled, soaping up his hands to lather up his body. He avoided scrubbing his arms so as not to wipe away the ink. The sex had been so fucking hot, but there was so much more to think about. Floyd was an old friend, an old partner, and the guy who was going to have his hands on him for something like forty hours in the next month.

They had to look each other in the eye today.

That didn't stop Greyson's exhausted body from burning, the blood still rushing around a little too freely – and down to his cock. The shower water hit the growing erection and streamed down around it in a little curtain of rain along his foot.

Greyson leaned against the shower wall and closed a soapy hand around his cock. He washed himself in a few quick strokes and swipes, running his thumb around the head, then let his hand close tightly around the shaft and stroke to the base.

He jerked off quick and hard to memories of Floyd's hot, tattooed body sprawled across the bed under him. He could viscerally remember Floyd's delicious, throbbing cock in his mouth, and he licked his lips with the craving he felt for the velvety heat again. The thick taste of Floyd's come was an echoed memory in the back of his throat. Then there were quick moments of his own fantasies: Floyd bending him in two to fuck him right back; Floyd's sure and certain hands running across his bare chest, pinching his nipples; Floyd's tongue licking into his mouth...

When Greyson came, he desperately tried to stifle his moan, but Floyd's name spilled over his lips anyway as he thrust his throbbing cock through his own tight fist.

He was almost dizzy from exertion and exhaustion by the time he was soft and he'd rinsed his cock and the shower clean. He stepped clear, toweling off and wrapping himself in the fluffy towel for a few moments to bask in those images again before he made himself forget them.

They hadn't even spent the night together, on Greyson's choice. Floyd might have woken up with regrets. Hell, he might not even want to acknowledge anything had happened. Greyson couldn't assume a damn thing yet.

His belly full of scrambled eggs, toast, bacon, and more, Greyson's nerves were far more settled. A big breakfast after a run was the best reward, and the best way of fueling up his muscles again. Especially since he was going to have to be strong today. He didn't know how much pain to expect.

Behind the tattoo shop counter, instead of the six-foot-odd man he'd pressed into the bed last night, was Chase. Jackson's boyfriend, he remembered from that pub meeting.

"Oh, hey," Greyson greeted, trying not to sound surprised. Chase worked here; of course he'd be here.

"Hi," Chase smiled. "Good to see you."

"What, Floyd not around? You on duty instead?" Greyson asked casually, hoping his worries weren't revealed by the easygoing question.

"He had to run the deposit to the bank," Chase told him. "Don't worry, he's still around to do your session. Sounds like a long one ahead of you guys." Chase's eyes were already on the inked outlines Floyd had so carefully drawn on Greyson yesterday. "Ohhh, *that'll* be something."

Greyson smiled, pulling his t-shirt sleeves up over his shoulders to show the tops of the designs. "Yeah, that's what I figured."

"Oh, man, let me see that. He showed me the outlines, but holy crap, it looks even better in person. You're gonna love that."

When Greyson approached and turned his arms this way and that for Chase to have a look, his stomach tensed – as usual. Chase didn't even seem to notice the scars, though. He must have been too busy following the contours of the outlines.

"It's not just outlined, is it?"

"No," Greyson assured him, shaking his head. "I just want to get everything done in even stages. I have an event in a month."

"Ahhh, right," Chase nodded. "Makes sense. So you know him, too, huh? From old days at work? He never talks about being a cop."

Greyson's mouth tightened and he leaned against the counter, looking out the door for Floyd instead of at Chase. "Yeah."

Chase hesitated for a few moments and chose not to comment. Instead, he said, "I'm glad he's meeting old buddies. I think he needs 'em."

"Yeah?" This was less dangerous turf, so Greyson looked over at Chase again. "He's got all of you guys, though, huh?"

Chase grinned. "Yeah, we hang out a lot. But he needs

more friends outside the business, too. One of our mutual friends just moved to Toronto to play hockey and Floyd's been moping. Don't tell him I said that..."

The idea of Floyd moping made Greyson chuckle fondly. He'd never seen him mope for some non-serious reason, so... it sounded kind of amusing. "Right. Everyone needs friends," he agreed. This was an awkward conversation at best, but Chase was trying.

"Speaking of which, you wanna come over for a barbecue next week? My boyfriend and his brothers liked hanging out with you too," Chase shrugged.

"As long as you don't expect me to fill in for that other guy and play hockey."

Chase laughed heartily. "No worries. I don't either. They tried to teach me and... it didn't go well for anyone. Even Noah's better."

The door rattled and Greyson smiled as Floyd entered. "Hey," Greyson nodded, then glanced back at Chase. "What day?"

"Thursday night? We usually barbecue on Thursdays. Come over anytime around supper."

"Sounds great."

When Greyson looked at Floyd again, Floyd's eyes were a little wide. It was like he couldn't believe Chase had made that offer. Then the look was gone and Floyd was smiling at him instead. "Hi."

Greyson ignored the weird moment. "Hey," he said again. "How's it going?"

"Pretty good. Ready to get started? I've got everything ready for you back there."

"Good luck," Chase smiled. "I'll leave you to it." He reached out for a handshake, which Greyson gave him.

"Thanks." Greyson pulled back from Chase to follow Floyd into the back room. His heart raced the moment they were left alone, though.

No hiding from him now.

"Take a seat and get your shirt off for me," Floyd told him, and his voice was exactly as professional as it had been yesterday.

Greyson decided to try his luck. "Yes, *sir.*" He swung his leg over the other side of the tattoo chair and flopped onto it, yanking his t-shirt off by the back of the neck. "And my pants?"

This made Floyd burst out laughing. "I think I can keep those clean."

"Damn," Greyson winked, stretching his arms out along the armrests as Floyd brought over alcohol wipes.

"So it'll be about twenty hours per arm, like I said before," Floyd refreshed his memory. "And I'm knocking the rate down to a hundred bucks an hour--"

"No, you don't have to," Greyson tried to interrupt, but Floyd waved him off.

"--since I owe you a lot. Old friend discount."

Greyson blinked a few times. *Is he saying what I think he's saying?* Greyson stayed quiet while Floyd sanitized his whole arm, then the other one. At last, Greyson cleared his throat. "So, about what you said..."

"You're not talking me out of the discount."

Greyson sighed and rolled his eyes. "You've always been a stubborn ass. I know that. No, I mean... you owe me?"

"I do." Floyd didn't seem to mind discussing it when he had something to keep his hands and eyes busy, like readying the tattoo machine. "I appreciate what you did for me all those years ago. In retrospect more than I did then, of course. I left Brett not long afterward."

Greyson let out a long sigh of relief. "Thank God." He meant it, too. "I was worried about... you know."

Floyd half-smiled. "Yeah. But I still don't think you handled it the right way." He paused as he rolled closer now, making direct eye contact with him.

Greyson nodded without hesitation. "I know."

Again, Floyd seemed surprised, but this time not in an unpleasant way. He hesitated, then rolled the rest of the way over. "So, it'll feel like a lot of stinging and shit. You know the drill. Tell me when it gets too much so we can both take a break, yeah? Don't go all macho bullshit on me."

"I'm half macho bullshit and half coffee. You know me. And I've only had two coffees," Greyson complained, just to make Floyd smile. Floyd *did* know his tendency to push through pain – like when he twisted his shoulder taking down a burglar but finished his shift despite Floyd's nagging.

It worked; Floyd grinned and shoved him lightly before adjusting his gloves and lowering the tattoo machine.

The first few pricks *did* sting, mostly because it was a kind of pain Greyson really wasn't familiar with.

"Ooof."

"You all right?"

"Yeah, fine," Greyson instantly reassured him. It was an indescribable sensation, and it lit his skin up with nervous energy. Yet there was a primal part of him that felt rooted to the ground and oh so alive. It was a feeling he'd been missing for *months*.

Oh, this is going to be the hardest thing I've ever done.

"God, things have changed now," Floyd laughed quietly, his gloved fingers tracing over his bicep. It was hard to keep his arm still and relaxed under the touch, but Greyson did his best to keep his fingers loose and breathing steady.

"Yeah," Greyson murmured. "I thought you'd hate me."

"Nah. I never did," Floyd shook his head. His eyes didn't flicker to Greyson's, though; he kept them firmly fixed on his work as he outlined with almost as much ease as he'd drawn yesterday. "I just resented that the department kept you safe."

Greyson's skin crawled with remembrance. One drunk night, a slip of the tongue, and he'd found out that Brett was bullying Floyd around. Brett was known at the station for getting into fights and shit, so there was no love lost on Floyd's boyfriend.

So, fueled by drink and rage, Greyson had gone to fix that.

Only Floyd hadn't been grateful after all. He'd been angry – furious – that the department kept Greyson utterly sheltered from consequences. Not that Brett had had the guts to try to challenge the cops over the coverup.

But Floyd had been heartbroken that justice could be doled out in other ways by those who were supposed to enforce it. Perhaps more distressed about that, even, than what had originally prompted Greyson to defend him.

Christ, Greyson couldn't stand bullies.

Slowly, with murmurs of conversation about ordinary things – sports first, then past tattoos, interesting cases Greyson had worked, and local news, the lines filled in. They snaked down from his shoulders to his wrists, the stark black ink embedded in reddening, stinging skin.

They took a break a couple hours in to grab sandwiches and drinks, then kept going.

The whole time, though, neither Greyson nor Floyd breathed a word about what had happened last night. It was comfortable that way, but Greyson's stomach churned more and more as their five-hour session drew to a close.

Floyd's hands running up and down his arms for hours conjured up the most pleasant body memories under his skin. It was hard not to get hard at the memory of Floyd's hands running up his arms, those soft hands cupping his cheeks... those *divine* lips on his...

The outlines were almost finished when their time was up. With the shading and coloring Floyd still had to do, Greyson could see why this was going to take such a long time.

Greyson steeled his courage as he lay back to wait to be bandaged, then turned his gaze to Floyd.

He had to know.

"This is kind of out of the blue now, but... do you want to go on a date? Or was last night... one time only?"

Floyd caught his breath in the middle of tearing off clear wrap, then finished ripping off the piece and rolled closer to wrap it around Greyson's forearm. "I... I wasn't expecting that," he admitted. "Yeah. I'd like that."

Greyson's shoulders sank slightly, and he offered a smile as the clear material clung to his skin before being taped up. "Cool. We'll text and work things out?"

"Yeah, sure." Floyd was being casual, but it didn't sound like he was blowing him off. It was more like he was trying to stay deliberately cool – maybe because this was such an awkward place between client and friend and lover.

Greyson hoped he hadn't made the next few weeks of sessions really weird.

CHAPTER
Eighteen
FLOYD

"Jesus, that was intense."

Floyd wiped down the tattoo chair absentmindedly, even though he'd done that twice already. Chase was leaning in the doorway watching him clean up after Greyson's session, and he could feel Chase's eyes boring into him.

"You look like you just had great sex," Chase laughed.

Floyd's head snapped around to Chase. "What? At work? That would break a few laws, I think--"

Chase was watching him with raised eyebrows, his lips pursed and hip jutting out to lean on the door frame.

Okay, now I'm acting weird and suspicious. Heat crept up Floyd's neck and then his cheeks, and he quickly strode over to wipe down the counter and check his ink supplies. "Sorry. Just, you know, licensing."

Chase nodded. "License renewal stressing you out?"

"Yeah."

Chase hummed, and he didn't sound convinced.

Floyd fought the exasperated frustration in his chest. It wasn't like he was doing an awesome job lying anyway.

"Okay, fine," Floyd muttered. "I know I'm on edge lately. Sorry."

"I was gonna say that," Chase nodded. He leaned back to glance down the hall toward the door as if checking that the shop was clear, then looked back at Floyd. "So, do you need advice or something?"

Floyd moved automatically to rinse the needle and put it in the ultrasonic cleaner, then checked the tattoo machine. That was sterilized, so he took it out to start reassembling it. The whole time, his mind churned over the question. He wasn't sure he wanted to recount the whole story right now.

"Seriously, man," Chase said, his voice quieter. "You helped me out before, when... you know."

When his family was stalking him. Creepy fuckers. "Right."

"I'm not interrogating you, but if you wanna talk, you know where I am."

Floyd met Chase's concerned gaze, then nodded as he shook his hands dry and grabbed the mop. "Thanks. I will."

Chase gave in and smiled, then strode up to the front again as the front door jangled to announce a new customer's arrival.

Floyd's mind wandered as he cleaned his station and the whole floor. He wasn't really sure where all of his tension was coming from, if he thought about it. This thing he had with Greyson was probably the least stressful part of it. Brett getting in touch again was pretty high up there, though.

He'd advised Chase to get some kind of exercise or take up self-defense or karate... any sport to feel more confident and burn off his energy. Chase had gone for fencing, and even the way he moved now was more confident.

Not that Floyd had confidence issues anymore, but walking to work and back was all the exercise he did these days. Plus, if he could get even a little bigger before the reunion next month...

"I need to get back to the gym," Floyd muttered under his breath, speaking aloud to hold himself to his promise. His archery arms were going to vanish at this rate. And there was one big bonus: a certain someone who worked at the gym. He'd get to see Greyson even more. Floyd was suddenly even more motivated.

It was time to deal with his tension the easiest possible way. Well, second-easiest. With Greyson in such close proximity, the easiest might happen again, though.

Floyd shivered with pleasure at the thought.

As he counted cash, Floyd glanced at his phone, which lay on the desk next to him.

Greyson had tipped him just right that afternoon, so he must have done his homework ahead of time. It felt weird to take money from him while flirting, but there was no chance in hell Greyson would let him discount his rate even more. Greyson had a lot more pride than was healthy.

His thoughts had been like this all day: while sweeping the waiting room, he'd thought about Greyson leaning on the counter; while selling body jewelry, he'd wondered why Greyson let his ear piercings heal over. He'd once had studs in each ear, and they'd looked damn hot on him.

Floyd couldn't help himself. He picked up the phone to send a quick text.

What time are your fitness classes?

He barely had the safe locked before he had an answer – a short listing of class times on each day of the week.

Floyd held his phone next to the week's schedule, his eyes flickering back and forth. He smiled when he noticed that he was off Friday evening, and Greyson was doing a class.

"Perfect. I can make that."

Then another idea occurred to him. If Greyson was still a fast healer like he once had been – bruises seemed to vanish within a day or two for him, an ability Floyd was jealous of – then he could tattoo every week.

Maybe every Friday evening, after class.

They could do the class together and shower together before they came to the studio...

He blushed, rubbing his cheeks for a moment before picking up his phone and locking up the office. Along the way, he answered.

Thanks. I can make it to your Friday class.

He had a response instantly.

Yes, would love to see you there. Before our next session?

Floyd laughed under his breath. Maybe Greyson was having the same thoughts.

Yeah. Your skin needs to be clean for the tattoo but we can shower together...

He hesitated before pressing send on the message. Was that too forward? Were they at the text-flirting stage yet?

"Fuck it." He hit send.

The answer came moments later.

;) Speaking of, when's the date?

Floyd grinned, tapping his phone against his chin for a moment. He pocketed it as he worked through his schedule in his head and locked up the shop, striding out once the security alarm was armed.

Then, Floyd answered as soon as he was on the street outside, the door securely locked.

Sunday afternoon lunch and walk?

He was off Sunday, so he could spend the whole day with him quite easily. Maybe he could do that regularly... Floyd liked the idea of a routine. Friday evening classes, Friday or Saturday tattoo sessions, Sunday dates...

Christ, we fucked once and I'm lining up my weekend schedule for two months, Floyd thought. He tried desperately to get the harebrained ideas out of his head.

Perfect :) Noon at the same cafe as before?

Yep :) Floyd answered, then tucked his phone away for the walk back home.

With thoughts of Greyson on his mind the whole time, he was barely in the apartment before he was picking up the phone again to text Kevin.

Hey Kev, I've got a real date now. Call me for the details :D

Floyd busied himself making supper as he waited for Kevin to have a minute to steal away after practice. It was hard keeping in touch with him, but he had no doubt Kevin would interrogate him as soon as humanly possible.

It had been way too long since he'd had a proper date when lunch and a walk sounded like the most romantic idea ever.

CHAPTER
Nineteen

GREYSON

"Here, put a label on this one."

"Sure." Greyson grabbed a marker to scrawl the car name and tire position on a piece of masking tape, then slapped it on the tire his dad had rolled in his direction.

"How's work going, then?" his dad asked as he tightened the lug nuts on the new summer tire.

It was a pretty safe topic of conversation. Greyson wheeled the tire to the back of the garage to stack with the others. "Can't complain. Classes are getting busy. Summer is workout season."

"I'd have thought people would be out exercising while it's warm out."

Greyson laughed. "No, it's just less awful to walk between the gym and the car this time of year."

His dad grunted, then eased himself up to do the next tire. They were almost done with this car, and then there was just one more – his mom's.

"Still thinking about becoming a cop again? I bet the force would hire you in a flash."

Greyson almost winced. He hadn't told his parents the real reasons for leaving Alberta – not all of them, at least. He'd hated it there and wanted to move back here, sure, but... he hadn't talked about the DV call.

"I'm sure they would," he lied, shrugging. "But I like the pace of life now."

"It must be a lot less stressful. Your mother and I figured you'd get out of it when you raised a family."

Greyson was avoiding that one like the plague. "Better hours, almost the same pay, a lot easier work, and it's less dangerous."

"Right," his father agreed. "But the benefits are better."

Greyson knew his dad wanted him back on the force, but at least he wasn't coming out and saying it. He'd always been proudest of him for being a man's man while he was a cop. And it had been his father's suggestion to go into it at all. His idea of fixing bullying was to learn to fight better.

It had worked, sort of. Greyson's confidence was higher than ever, but then he'd gone and seen – and done – enough shit for one lifetime in a few years.

Being a first responder wasn't something he was ever going to feel good about. His guilt about that one mistake—that huge mistake—here in Fredericton overshadowed his pride about the work he'd done in Alberta. It was a dark cloud over his record. Thinking about it only aggravated the itch under his skin to absolve that guilt.

Greyson didn't answer, and his father didn't say anything more except to ask for wrenches or swap tires with him.

When they were done, Greyson moved with his dad to the house for lunch. He'd had his long-sleeved shirt on to make sure the freshly healing skin stayed clean. That was another discussion he had to have with them today.

"All done? Wash up and let's have sandwiches and soup."

That was his mother, still younger and more energetic than his dad. She tended to be understanding of him, if not overly warm. Neither of his parents really were, though.

"Thanks." Greyson was careful as he pushed up his sleeves to wash his hands, wincing at the tender skin underneath. Then, he carefully rolled up the sleeves to be a little tidier at the dinner table. Black outlines of mountains peeked out from under the rolled fabric.

Naturally, he hadn't even had a few bites of his sandwich before his parents noticed. "Is that a temporary tattoo?" his father frowned, reaching out to poke toward his wrist.

"Afraid not," Greyson smiled. "I'm getting sleeves done."

There was a moment of silence before his mother nodded. "Well, I didn't see that coming, but it's your own decision."

"No regulations on what you can get done if you're working at the gym, I suppose," his father agreed.

Greyson's jaw twitched in irritation but he nodded nonetheless. "And I'm liking it there, too. They're adding another class a week to my schedule next week."

"That's great." His mother still kept looking at his forearms, so Greyson sighed and gently pushed his sleeves up. He tried not to rub the material against the tattoos, though there had been constant stinging all day from exactly that. He didn't let them look for long at his inside arms, just the outsides of his forearms. "They'll go all the way up."

Though both his parents murmured their approval, he could tell it was lukewarm at best.

Oh, well. This was something *he* needed.

His mother went with the tried-and-true segue within

minutes, just as he finished his soup. "So, have you met anyone yet?"

Greyson snorted with laughter and shook his head. "Well..." *I'm not telling them anything close to all about it.* "I have met someone I like. That's about all, though. No news yet."

"Oh, that's new, though. We haven't heard of anyone since you moved back here."

His father nodded. "It's good for you to meet people and make friends, if your old buddies aren't going to be around."

Not telling him that Darren and Lyle are the only ones who still wanna talk to me.

Greyson's stomach twisted, but he smiled anyway. "Yeah, yeah, of course," he agreed. "You know Jackson Riley, the blacksmith who did your friends' railings over on..." he gestured, trying to remember their names.

"Sharon and her husband, yes. Lovely couple."

"Yes, them. I met him and the rest of his family not long ago, and they invited me to come over and chat. They seem like a good bunch. There's a lot of them, too."

"Mmm." His mother looked intrigued as she watched him, but she didn't ask any more questions yet. He could just *see* her putting two and two together, though. Not that they didn't know he was gay... but they might not have expected him to "still" be gay, per se. "I see."

"Good," his father said again, standing to gather the dishes. "As long as you're not getting tattooed to fit in with the crowd."

Greyson rocked back on his chair for a moment from sheer surprise, then laughed hard as all four legs hit the ground again. "I'm a *little* past that stage, thanks, Dad."

"You can never be too sure," his mother nodded, and then the conversation moved on to her plants and yard work.

That hadn't actually gone too badly. That was the advantage of Greyson's parents having always been a little too distant: telling them anything was easy. He could have it a lot worse.

CHAPTER
Twenty
FLOYD

WHY THE FUCK WAS HIS PHONE RINGING ON SUNDAY morning?

Shit, had he slept in?!

Floyd sat bolt upright and fought the covers away from his arms so he could grab the phone from his bedside table. He squinted at it, confused to see an incoming call instead of an alarm.

He tapped the answer button and raised his phone to his ear, rolling onto his side and then his front. "Hello?" he murmured, not even trying to disguise his sleep-roughened voice.

"I thought you'd never wake up. Good morning."

It was his mother.

"Morning." Floyd resisted the urge to sigh, just rolled his eyes as hard as he could without straining them. He sat slowly up again, then eased his feet out of bed to stand up and stretch.

"I need you to run me around to a few stores. They didn't

tell me the leather wasn't going to stretch because of the way the seam was put together--"

Floyd tuned out the rant as he walked to his window, yanking the blinds open.

A gorgeous day for a walk with Greyson, thank God.

There was no chance to wait for a pause. "I can't run you around today," Floyd interrupted. "I have plans today. I could have if you'd told me earlier..."

"What?" His mother sounded taken aback, to say the least, and no surprise. He'd done just about everything she'd asked for months – years – trying to make up for those lost years. "So you're just saying no?"

"I can't," Floyd said again, keeping his tone carefully neutral. "I can rearrange my schedule and do it tomorrow, though."

"Always making excuses, like you weren't raised better," his mother muttered, and he could hear clanging dishes in the background. Then a cupboard or door slammed. "Fine, your father will rearrange his life to do it."

It wasn't like she didn't have a driver's license. She just opted not to use it.

"Okay. Talk to you later this week," Floyd answered, refusing to fall for the bait. She hung up first, and he sighed, pressing his phone to his face for a moment before tossing it on the bed hard.

God, he hated being the one to say no, but his date with Greyson? He wasn't passing that up for the world.

With that thought in mind, Floyd's mood turned pleasant again and he smiled all the way to the shower.

"Hey!"

Floyd was taken aback when he heard Greyson's voice, and it took him a moment to place him. When he did, he smiled. Greyson was leaning against the wall near the restaurant, and he'd walked right by him, lost in his own thoughts.

Oops. Get it together, man.

"How's it going?" Floyd greeted, keeping his tone light. God, Greyson was hot. The way his shirt stretched over his biceps, tucked perfectly into his jeans... It was ten times worse now that he knew about those washboard abs underneath. He could see the subtle ripples in the fabric where it pulled tight across his sculpted body.

Greyson raised his eyebrow. "Better now that you're around," he winked, and God, the charm just oozed from every fiber of his being.

And Floyd lapped it up. "Let's find a seat," Floyd answered, but he knew his cheeks were burning.

"How was your day?"

"Er... not long since we've seen each other," Floyd laughed. "Nothing interesting happened." *Just that call from my mother, and that's hardly interesting.*

Greyson nodded as he held the door open for Floyd, and Floyd smelled his distinctive musk – mossy and leather and just a little lavender – tickling his nose. Worse yet, his shoulder brushed against Greyson's broad chest, and tingling warmth spread through his whole body in a flash.

Oh, Jesus, he wanted to be in Greyson's strong arms again.

"Table for two, please." Once they were seated, Floyd distracted himself. "S-So, what about your day?" he asked, a bit too brightly. "Did anything interesting happen?"

"Not much. I went to see my parents. Swapped out the winter tires for summer ones."

"Oh, that's exciting." Floyd made a face, and Greyson laughed. "I mean, unless you're into mechanical stuff..."

"Not really," Greyson shrugged. "But it's something my dad and I can do together."

"Right." Floyd watched him for a moment, trying not to get pulled in by the way his lips pursed, or his broad hands fidgeted with the lunch menu...

He's so gorgeous. And he knows it. Floyd couldn't get sucked in by the man's incessant charm. Greyson had a dad who helped him change his tires, for God's sakes. He'd drag him into his weird family dynamics and recovery process and all that shit.

And if they broke up... this time, going not just from partners to nothing, but from *partners* to nothing...

His mental state was going to be fucked up again.

Sure, last time was getting out an abusive relationship while losing his work partner and quitting his job... but he didn't want to go through anything like that again. Even if his life was just slow and steady, at least he knew what it would bring him.

It didn't stop his heart from fluttering as he watched Greyson order, the friendly smile on his lips and the deeply-ingrained politeness that made him nod several times as he handed back the menu.

"O-Oh, uh... What he's having."

Shit. He was crushing like a fucking teenager, forgetting his order and getting entranced by just watching the way he moved.

What was wrong with him?

Floyd kept the conversation as light as he could until

their food came out and they dug in. It was nice to have company while he ate, though. He'd forgotten how much he missed that since his last relationship. God, when was that?

He'd made a few attempts at them since dumping Brett, but none had lasted long.

"Penny for your thoughts?"

Floyd smiled apologetically and shook his head. "Sorry, I totally spaced out there. What were you saying before about, uh, Alberta... gardens?"

"Just different, being back here and seeing... you know, all the cute little houses and their cute little yards. It's a nice atmosphere here." Greyson was watching him, those dark eyes too perceptive by far. "D'you like it?"

"I like it enough to stick around here," Floyd shrugged his agreement. "I never really felt the pull of the big city. I mean, some of my friends like Chase came here just to get away from the fast pace. But I know a lot more people who are leaving."

"That's kind of sad, when you put it that way," Greyson laughed. "Like me. But they'll be back when they're ready to settle down and start a family..."

Then, it was Greyson's turn to pause, his almost automatic charm interrupted by a moment of embarrassment. His cheeks were red as he grabbed his water glass.

Can't resist. "So, are you looking for a nice hubby and kids?" Floyd teased, leaning back in his seat and grinning as Greyson's eyes dropped to the table with embarrassment. "Came back here to find them?"

"I – someday, yeah," Greyson said, his voice even hesitating. "I'm not opposed to the idea."

"Which one?"

"Both."

Floyd smiled, then leaned forward a little. "I want them, too. But not yet."

"God, no," Greyson laughed quickly, seemingly glad to move past this. He pushed back his dishes while Floyd did the same. "So, up for that walk yet?"

"Sure," Floyd grinned. He still had Greyson's embarrassment stuck in his head. It was like he hadn't wanted to admit that to anyone – or like he hadn't even thought about it himself.

Their hands were *nearly* brushing by the time they reached the park. Floyd's nerves were crackling with impatient hunger while he desperately tried to focus on Greyson's words.

Greyson's hands were tucked into his pockets as he wandered alongside Floyd. They'd crossed the walking bridge to the other side of the river, and they were wandering up the trail. Floyd had never walked this far out, but it felt like nothing alongside Greyson.

"A surprising number of skills transfer over from the force to fitness," Greyson was telling him. "Being able to assess people's builds and mannerisms quickly, place their type. Assess their reactions. Most of all, know when they're hurting themselves or when they're not pushing hard enough."

Floyd shifted, a knot twisting in his stomach. He'd never felt easy about the skills he'd taken from his own brief stint in the force – training, then four months of service until the incident. Plus, afterward, a month of bitter resentment until the slow slide downhill into drinking and feeling sorry for himself.

"Sorry," Greyson added after a moment, his voice uncertain now. "I keep forgetting it was so long ago for you."

Floyd shook his head. "Feels like yesterday sometimes."

"I miss it."

"I don't." Floyd's words were harder than he'd intended, his voice steely.

Greyson looked at him for a few moments, his expression hard to read, but there was a wrinkle between his brows and he wasn't leaning into him. Then, he looked away and hummed, dropping the subject. "Should we turn around? I don't know what lies this far out."

"The north side, so mysterious."

"By foot, it is," Floyd laughed. "I walk around downtown, not this far out." He pivoted with Greyson to walk back toward the bridge. "I suppose you had better trails out in Alberta."

Greyson shrugged. "Some. I didn't get out much."

"Mm." Floyd gestured toward Greyson's arms. "So, everything healing fine?" He'd chosen a long-sleeved shirt with thin, loose sleeves, which was a wise decision.

"Oh, yeah." Greyson unbuttoned one of his sleeves, and Floyd's skin tingled with desire. He pushed it aside to focus on Greyson's reddened, yet clearly healing skin. The outlines looked crisper now.

Floyd raised his eyebrows. "Jeez, you still do heal fast." He looked like he'd had it done a couple days ago now, not just yesterday.

Greyson half-smiled. "I know." His eyes flickered as he pushed his sleeve back down. "Anyway, you should come to a class. You hinted at it before."

"A group one?" Floyd touched his hair in thought, running a hand back and forth over the close-cropped hairs at the back of his neck. He'd just decided the other day to do it, so this was his chance to follow through. "Okay. The one next Friday..."

"How about sooner? A one-on-one session, free?"

"Uh-uh," Floyd shook his head, shoving Greyson's side while being careful not to jostle his arm. "You pay for my services, I pay for yours."

"The first session's usually free," Greyson informed him with a smug grin.

Floyd eyed Greyson, then shook his head. He couldn't argue that. "Okay, but the other ones aren't. We'll work out a trade for the tattoo time versus training time. How about Wednesday?"

This was way more than tattoos for training, or even than a date for the reunion.

Greyson laughed. "Sure." He looked even more self-satisfied. "Perfect."

They were back at Floyd's car now, and Floyd leaned on the door handle. "So..."

"So, this was nice," Greyson commented, his smile simple and direct. "Can we do it again?"

Floyd nodded. He couldn't remember such an enjoyable Sunday afternoon. The only way to make it better... well, he couldn't invite him home again so soon, could he? *No, knock it off.* "Definitely. Maybe next weekend."

"Great," Greyson murmured, stepping closer. He slid a hand onto Floyd's waist, then stepped between his feet to close the gap between them.

Floyd easily let go of the car and rested his own hands carefully on those powerful hips. He tried not to think about what they were capable of. He leaned in until their lips met, then slid slowly along each other. Soft, passionate kisses swept him along on a tide of desire until Floyd pulled back.

"See you soon." Floyd managed to keep his voice steady, which amazed even him, but the moment Greyson's hands slid away from him, he was left colder than he'd realized. The warmth of even walking next to him wasn't to be underestimated.

Greyson looked delicious standing there in his black leather jacket, dark red collared shirt, and dark jeans that showed off every inch of his muscled legs and great ass. Floyd dragged his eyes back to Greyson's face and gave a quick wave, then circled around to the driver's side.

By the time he pulled away, Greyson was climbing into his own car, but the image of Greyson standing on the sidewalk watching after him wasn't going to leave his mind any time soon.

And he still tasted Greyson's warm, soft lips.

God, he wanted this man.

CHAPTER
Twenty~One
GREYSON

"RIGHT IN THE MIDDLE! THAT'S MY BOY!"

Greyson's back straightened with pride at his father's exclamation from the other side of the bar. The double bull meant an easy victory for him. He eyed the dart board for a moment, then walked over to collect his darts.

"Oh, Jesus," Mark exclaimed, slapping his back on the way by in both congratulations and condemnation. "Dave, your boy here's got us beat."

Greyson grinned at him. "Your go."

The rest of the round was lazy. His dad's buddies, Mark, Andrew, and Hugh, didn't even want to try against him.

The atmosphere here was laid-back. Everyone seemed welcoming, even when Greyson had shown up for the first time in years a few months ago. Sometimes his dad came to the bar too, and sometimes not. Most of the guys knew his dad better than him, but they all respected him for his former career.

The round was done as fast as that, and Greyson laid

down his darts. He sat down to finish the rest of his beer, tuning into the conversations nearby.

"...near the fairy grove. Just down the street from them."

Greyson's shoulders rose and he fought to keep his expression neutral. He knew exactly who that referred to, but he played dumb as he turned to his dad. "From who now?"

"You know, the brothers."

"Which brothers?"

"The Rileys."

"Fairy Grove? Is that the neighborhood?"

His father rolled his eyes and flagged down another beer from the bartender. "Oh, don't get politically correct with me."

Hugh was laughing in the background while Mark eyed Greyson for his reaction.

Don't let them get a rise. Greyson just raised his eyebrow. "Everyone bitches about Alberta being stuck in the seventies-_"

"Oh, don't take it so seriously," his father laughed. "Anyway, you heard of that new corner store? Butch and his kid are supposed to be running it..."

Greyson tuned out again as his father started talking more to Mark, Jeff, and the other half-dozen guys within earshot, just gazing across the bar to idly watch the TV. The game was some minor league clash, but not Toronto. Otherwise he would have been much more interested.

"What?"

His father was jostling him, gesturing across the room to the pretty young woman seated on the other side of the bar. This bar was the rare type that made women feel comfortable even though there were dart boards and sports TVs. It was easy to flirt here, and the bartenders kept an eye out for anyone who was putting on too much pressure.

"What about her?"

"She looks like your type."

Greyson gave him a flat stare of disbelief, unable to hide the pinching of his brows. "Really?"

His dad turned to Hugh and Mark. "Doesn't she?"

How the fuck would you remember my type? Years ago, he'd flirted with women to keep up appearances – before he'd been free from everyone, free enough to choose his own adventure. He didn't think he'd shown that much interest in any one woman.

"Yeah, go buy her a drink. Chat her up." That was Jeff, in the background, leaning around Mark. "She looks your age."

Greyson cut a glare back to his father as the other guys chimed in with their agreement, then jerked his chin to the side, near the wall, where nobody was sitting. He grabbed his beer bottle and strode over there, ignoring the 'ooh's from the other guys.

"What's your problem?" he hissed, his voice low. "First you bust out that old fairy shit again, and then you're trying to set me up with some chick?"

His dad seemed blithely unconcerned as he sipped his beer. "I thought she seemed your type anyway."

"*She* did? *She?*" Greyson emphasized, and he knew he was glaring now, but he didn't care. It was petty of his father to do whatever the fuck this was, and he was going to be petty right back.

"What about that girl back when you were a cop? The other cop? I thought the two of you..."

Greyson had to search his mind, but of course, it didn't take long. There had only been one other unmarried woman his own age – Mandy, who'd worked traffic. His father had seen them at the ceremonies and got stuck on the idea of his police son marrying a policewoman. Making the perfect police family.

Even back then, Greyson had known it wasn't right.

His father did, too, as stubbornly as he tried to ignore it. Greyson shook his head with a derisive snort. "No. Just... no." He gulped down the last few sips of beer and set it down on the table nearby with a scoff.

He wanted another drink before he headed home. He wasn't going to storm out on that note; everyone else would know *something* was up. So Greyson swallowed his pride, turning his back on his dad to head back to the bar and order another. Then his dad was back in his chair, too, like nothing had ever happened.

The others let it blow over, even if he saw a few curious looks. No doubt some of them thought he had some secret girlfriend now. Or else they suspected the truth.

Greyson's shoulders hunched slightly as he rested his elbows on the bar, his chest rising and falling a little faster. It wasn't like he was ashamed. And they weren't gonna take him out back and beat him or anything. But...

But then there were little snide comments, the feigned innocence during cruel jokes, the laughter behind his back.

He didn't want to put up with that shit.

Greyson chatted to the others when they talked to him, but he couldn't keep it up for much longer. When he finished that beer he headed out with a wave, laughing and rolling his eyes when he was accused of leaving before the others could outscore him in the next darts game.

The smile dropped off his face the moment he was out in

the dark parking lot, kicking at each piece of gravel that skittered across pavement on his route home.

He really needed another beer... or six.

Greyson hadn't felt an urge this strong in months. His stomach was tight, his fingers fidgety, and he couldn't focus on anything for more than a few seconds. Anxiety burned under his skin, the flames fueled higher the more he tried to ignore it.

It was like he couldn't contain himself, he was crawling slowly out of his skin and up the wall.

Or like he couldn't breathe, couldn't quite feel himself and know it was him.

Words failed him, but he knew what the sensation meant: he needed to be grounded. He needed to feel *real* again. And the easiest way...

"No," Greyson whispered, letting out a slow breath. He wasn't going to relapse now – not over his fresh tattoos, and not on his thighs or anywhere else, damn it. He'd been fighting this for too long to slip.

Besides, he knew someone who would want to help.

Can we hang out tonight?

He hovered over Floyd's last message, rereading the chain, then pressed "send" before he chickened out.

Floyd's response came within a minute.

Yeah, I had a shitty day and I want company. You?

Me too.

Greyson smiled slightly. He wasn't happy that Floyd was unhappy, but it was kind of nice not to have to pretend to be happy and shit around him. Floyd knew... at least the bare bones of his situation, but still...

It was hard to pretend all the time, but even harder to let control slip and let someone in.

Greyson's phone went off again with another text from Floyd. This one was simple.

Come over?

On my way.

Everything felt like it took much too long, but Greyson hauled himself to his feet and changed into a nicer shirt, then set off for the quick drive to Floyd's apartment.

"Come on in."

Greyson smiled at the sight of Floyd in a t-shirt and casual, ripped jeans. He'd clearly been lounging about, too. The faint pattern of tattoos peeking through the rips on his jeans was downright hot, but he dragged his eyes back up to Floyd's face as he walked into the apartment.

The living room was spacious and bright, and best of all, familiar to Greyson. He crashed next to Floyd on the couch once his shoes were off, stretching his arms along the back of the sofa. Greyson nodded at the TV, which was playing an obnoxious medication commercial. "What's on?"

"Really nothing," Floyd laughed. "Just watching sports."

"What kind?"

"Baseball."

Greyson made a face, and Floyd's laugh this time was startled but sincere. "You don't like baseball?" Floyd asked.

"No... I've always thought it's boring as crap," Greyson shrugged. "Hockey, football, soccer, rugby, curling..."

"Curling?" Floyd snorted. "I used to do that as a kid."

Greyson smirked. Somehow, he wasn't terribly surprised. "Really? Were you any good?"

Floyd mumbled, "Not at all." He turned back to the TV and flipped up a few channels to find a hockey game rerun.

"I'd be bad at it too, I'm sure," Greyson grinned. "I never knew that. Were you uncoordinated or did you have bad aim? Or did you not sweep intensely enough?"

"Fuck off," Floyd laughed. "I bet you only played manly sports."

"Hockey for a bit," Greyson nodded. "I wasn't as bulky as the other kids, though... Jesus, these days it's bad. They bring their kids into the gym for training at ten, eleven years old, to make sure they get bigger. Even back then, it wasn't that bad. You just accepted you'd get slammed around a little more. You remember me back in high school. By then I was out, it was only the pros or wanna-be pros still doing it. Heh, it'll be weird seeing them again... seeing if any of them actually pursued it."

Their knees brushed, and Floyd was leaning back against his arm. Even though it stung slightly, Greyson ignored it and didn't pull back from him. Instead, he shifted so the sides of their thighs lightly pressed.

Floyd rubbed his hair, half-watching the TV and half-watching Greyson. "Did you suspect even then?"

"The gay thing? Nah," Greyson shrugged. Then, he hesitated. "Well..."

Floyd smirked, an "aha" expression on his face. "Mm?"

"There were a few other guys I admired... a lot..."

Floyd laughed. "Yeah, me too. Then I realized I wanted to fuck them or be fucked by them."

"Took me a long time to work that one out," Greyson shook his head. "I'm kinda glad I didn't really know back then, or things *would* have been more awkward. But everyone else guessed years before me anyway." He'd never really had a chance to be in the closet to anyone else – just himself, and maybe his family. But half of that was them being stubborn shitheads about it.

Floyd chuckled. "I didn't. Didn't see that coming at all." He licked his lips unconsciously, and God, they were so fucking kissable.

"That's what he said," Greyson smirked, unable to resist the tease. Floyd rolled his eyes at him and shook his head. "Sorry."

"You haven't changed a bit. It's just *he* instead of *she* now, isn't it?" Floyd grinned.

Greyson laughed and half-shrugged. He'd always been a smooth talker; he'd just never gotten the chance to direct his attention to Floyd before now. "Maybe."

Floyd's eyes flickered down to Greyson's lips for a moment, then back up to his eyes. "Good thing I like that." He shook his head, like he was trying to put something out of his head and focus on Greyson.

Greyson slid his arm forward, until it properly rested against Floyd's shoulders, around the back of his neck, his fingers wrapped around Floyd's upper arm. That brought Floyd's attention to a single point – him. "You're a sucker for a sweet-talker."

Floyd shifted so their thighs pressed together harder, warmth shooting through Greyson at the close contact and the way Floyd was watching him. "God, am I ever."

I need to get my mind off shit. It sounds like he does, too. Greyson leaned in slowly, giving Floyd time to anticipate it, and Floyd met him halfway. Their lips melded together in a crash of warmth and desire.

It took seconds before Greyson's skin was burning with need. His breath caught roughly in his throat. His cock stirred to life, along with his desire to push Floyd down on the sofa and press himself between those hot thighs.

"Yes!" Floyd moaned through the kiss in a feverish mumble, then gasped when Greyson caught his lip and sucked it lightly. Greyson loved the way Floyd's breathing stuttered before he mumbled something else.

"Hm?" Greyson murmured, pulling back just enough to breathe against the wet, sensitive skin.

Floyd gasped, "I said, I wanna suck you."

Fire burst under Greyson's skin, his cock instantly throbbing in his pants at the thought of those beautiful, broad lips pursed around the tip of his cock. "Oh, yeah."

"Cool." Floyd slithered out from under his arm, squirming against his hold until he managed to slide to the floor. Greyson promptly squeezed his shoulders, then cupped his cheeks.

Floyd pressed his lips against Greyson's denim-clad inner thigh, but the jeans were thick enough that he could only barely feel warm pressure. It was a fucking tease this way. "You look so hot from down here."

It was hard for Greyson to reconcile his mental image of himself with Floyd's sincere words. Floyd's pupils were huge as he stared at Greyson like he was the hottest thing in the *world*. Greyson's cheeks flushed with heat and he looked away for a moment.

Normally, he could take a compliment, and he knew objectively that guys found him hot. That was how he got laid so easily.

Floyd mistook it as an attempt to control his arousal. "I love making you lose control." He kissed up Greyson's leg to his crotch, then the bulge forming in the front of his jeans. "I love the look on your face when you come. I love the way your cock tastes."

Greyson easily remembered last time: Floyd's hot mouth around him, Floyd's skilled tongue lapping around his head and sucking his swollen rod down into his throat.

"But this time," Floyd whispered, his voice harsh as he unbuttoned Greyson's jeans and yanked them down enough to get his hard cock out into the air, "I wanna finish you off this way."

Greyson gasped. The hot erection stood out in cool air for only a moment before Floyd's broad, talented hand was wrapping around the shaft, pushing a tight ring down to the base. "Christ. O-Okay." Floyd was stubborn and determined, like he knew exactly what he wanted, and it made Greyson even hotter.

Floyd's tongue trailed up along the underside of the shaft, and then down the seam between his balls.

"F-Fuck!" Greyson's breathing was even harsher now as he writhed into the sofa, spreading his knees further apart. Floyd's talented tongue swiped around each of his balls, then up the bottom of the shaft all the way to the tip.

Floyd hummed against the flesh, then slid his pursed lips around the shaft in a quick burst of wet warmth.

This sensation never got old. Greyson hummed, then moaned his pleasure as Floyd's pursed lips slid slowly down his shaft to the base and back up again, enveloping all of him with the beautiful pressure. He kneaded Floyd's shoulders, his head rolling back against the back of the couch.

"Mmmm," Floyd moaned around his cock, his tongue swiping back and forth across the head and around it. The vibrations made Greyson gasp and twitch, his thighs tensing up for a second. Floyd noticed the reaction and moaned again, his teeth very lightly grazing the shaft.

"Yes...!" Greyson gasped, his body briefly tensing and shuddering. That particular controlled burn was *always* ten times better than he remembered.

Floyd sucked the head of his cock down into his throat and swallowed a few times, his throat muscles working around him, and Greyson was almost out of his mind with pleasure. Not only could he talk dirty like a pro, but he could deep-throat him.

Oh, Christ, Greyson was so fucking close to coming already. Floyd's lips and tongue and cheeks and teeth... Every part of him worked on Greyson for his pleasure.

When Greyson glanced down to watch his own swollen, reddened shaft sliding back and forth across those supple lips, he was startled to find Floyd's eyes on him. The wide hazel eyes were fixed on his every expression and reaction.

Somehow, that was even hotter than any other single detail of the experience.

"Christ," Greyson whispered, unable to tear his eyes away from Floyd's face now. He tangled his hand in the hair at the back of Floyd's head, the nails of his other hand biting into Floyd's muscled shoulder. He was so close...

Floyd sucked his lips back up to the tip and wrapped his hand around the shaft to squeeze and stroke while he sucked the tip hard.

Greyson's body tensed, his head slamming into the back of the couch while his hips shoved up and his cock pulsed his pleasure. His whole body tightened and released unconsciously and he was gone, swept away on the tide of pleasure.

"Y-Yes...! Floyd, fuck, yes..." Greyson moaned, and Floyd

just kept steadily licking around the head and sucking it firmly.

He couldn't look away from Floyd for a second, well aware that Floyd was drinking in every second of his orgasm just as much as the hot pleasure that pulsed from his cock. Only when he had to squeeze his eyes shut did he do so.

Even then, he quickly looked back at Floyd when the blackness cleared again from his thoughts and vision. "Oh," Greyson groaned, his hips shoving forward a few more times to get the last few shivers out of the way before he flopped back on the couch with a gasp.

"Mmm," Floyd moaned. He pulled away, his throat working as he swallowed, then grinned. "You're very noisy."

Greyson's cheeks were already flushed from the heat, but they prickled again. He mumbled, "Yeah, sometimes. When I'm getting the best blowjob ever."

"Compliment accepted," Floyd teased, rocking back onto his heels. He wasn't quick to rise to his feet, still crouching there and gazing up the length of Greyson's body. "Christ, that was hot. *You're* hot."

Greyson shoved Floyd's shoulder lightly and laughed. "Get back up here." He carefully tucked himself back in his underwear and hauled his jeans back up, buttoning them up one-handed.

When Floyd crashed next to him, Floyd's arm went around his shoulders instead. Greyson hated to admit it, but he felt safer than ever in Floyd's hold.

They held each other for a minute, and Greyson reached out to try to feel up Floyd's thigh. Floyd just pushed his hand away with a smile and shake of his head. "I'm fine."

Greyson nodded, then leaned into Floyd's side again,

half-closing his eyes as he watched the game. They stayed like this for a minute in contented silence.

Floyd finally murmured, "You wanna stay over?"

Greyson shook his head, but he smiled at Floyd anyway. He just wanted to be in his own bed again, but he was starting to feel the pull to have Floyd there with him, too. "I'll be okay on my own." The gnawing anxiety under his skin was gone for now.

It wasn't even the sex. It had vanished the moment he'd seen Floyd's friendly face opening the door.

"I'll see you Wednesday for our one-on-one session, right?"

Greyson snorted. "I hope so. Don't skip out on me."

Floyd laughed. "Quitting before I start? Not a chance."

"Good. Come ready to work out," Greyson teased.

He stayed until the end of the game before hauling himself up to his feet again, his skin still pleasantly tingling from the pleasant, easy company. Around Floyd, it was so easy to be himself – even when he was low-energy. Every time, Floyd left him smiling and thinking about the next time they were going to see each other.

He's an addiction, and the best kind for me.

CHAPTER
Twenty~Two
FLOYD

"Excuse me – is Greyson in?"

The blond receptionist glanced up at Floyd, his eyebrows raised. "Right. He was expecting someone. He's over in the back weight room."

"Thanks." Floyd brushed off his workout clothes and turned to take in the gym. He wasn't exactly scrawny, but it was easy to feel self-conscious among guys who actually hit the gym every day.

He thought he saw the blond guy's eyes on him for a moment, but when he glanced back, he was looking away with a little smile. It was kind of nice to be hit on, even if he wasn't interested in it.

Floyd strode to the weight room, trying to ignore the burly dudes watching themselves in the mirror as they slowly curled their biceps and triceps, and shit. It was a lot easier to ignore them when he saw Greyson there in a tight little t-shirt setting up racks of weights. "Hey. Ready to train the newbie?"

Greyson straightened up and grinned. "So ready. Ready to learn?"

"Yes, teacher," Floyd winked. It was a bit unnerving to see himself in the mirrors lining the room, and it made his imagination wander to all kinds of dirtier possibilities. He tried to put them out of mind, though.

Greyson's shoulder blades bulged through the back of his shirt as he turned to grab a set of weights for himself, spinning them casually in his hands. "How are you?"

"Great." Floyd could hardly keep his eyes on Greyson's face now that he'd noticed his shorts stretching tight around his muscled thighs. "Just great. You?"

Greyson smirked as he approached, still idly turning the weights this way and that. "Good. Here, grab these."

Floyd wrapped his hands around the cylindrical handles, the weights dropping to his thighs before he adjusted for the weight and lifted them again. "A bit heavy, but that's all right."

"Good. They should be a strain, but not much of one." Greyson stayed close to him. He was just half a pace closer than average, but Floyd had no idea how personal space worked here. "Let's see. What do you need to know...? Ah, right. Here, I'll show you the three basic positions we'll be using..."

Floyd swallowed hard, keeping his eyes on his own form in the mirror and trying not to watch Greyson's ass in it instead. Greyson wrapped his hand around the handle to guide Floyd's motion. "Up this way, breathe... that's it. Remember to breathe. And down this way, in a controlled motion, making it as slow as you can handle. And when you have your arm out this way, up and down like this..."

Floyd's cheeks were flushed with heat from the amusement of trying to bite back his comments. He glanced around in the mirror, glad nobody was too close to them.

"And in and out, if we're lucky," Greyson whispered, then took a step back. "Perfect. You're set."

Floyd's lips parted, and he saw himself blush in the mirror. "Mm..."

Greyson abruptly pulled back from him, clapping his shoulder on the way by to the door. "Get familiar with the weights. I'll be back in a minute."

Floyd let out a breath and tried to keep himself calm, watching his form as he moved the free weights up and down at different angles. He'd lifted weights years ago with buddies in cop training, but not since then.

The place was quiet right now, at least. This room seemed a little smaller than the weight room closer to the front, with less fancy gear, but that meant it drew less people. Floyd preferred it already.

"Right," Greyson said as he approached, clapping his hands and grabbing weights for himself. "Have a seat."

Floyd settled into the familiar position with his spine against the backrest, his body settling into a comfortable, safe form. It was pure muscle memory, since he hadn't done it in years. Listening to Greyson's instructions came on automatic as they did reps and sets with a few different weights.

"Your form's just fine. You remember your gym time, huh?"

Floyd nodded, out of breath but starting to feel high off the burn in his arms and chest. "Yeah, more than I expected."

"You can up your weights with your form looking so good."

"I can't handle more yet," Floyd snorted. "Start me slow."

"You're not even breaking a sweat. Trust me." Greyson

hopped up from his bench, setting down his own weights and grabbing Floyd's to swap them out for weights that were a couple pounds heavier.

Floyd made a face. Greyson was right – he was being a wuss, but he didn't want to embarrass himself by failing halfway through a set. He'd just have to steel himself.

Halfway through the set, Greyson smacked him in the stomach.

"Oof!" Floyd nearly dropped the weights. "You asshole."

Greyson laughed. "You're not breathing."

"I-- oh." Floyd settled back again, trying to remember to breathe in and out now as he lifted until his muscles screamed.

The other guys had left, and they were the only two in the room right now, but even so, Greyson didn't try to get closer like Floyd had half-expected. He was just keeping a close eye on Floyd, presumably making sure he wasn't in legitimate medical distress.

"Where do you feel the burn the most?"

"Biceps and pecs and... something in my back I didn't know I had," Floyd grumbled.

Greyson smirked. "Oh, the first time I carried weights while I ran--"

Floyd stared. Weights while he ran? "Oh God, that sounds even more stupidly healthy," he interrupted. "I'll never keep up."

"Don't try to keep up," Greyson laughed, setting his weights down at last. "Okay, you're done. Man, you're good considering. I run every morning for fun, and then I work out here. It's half my day. You're busy doing delicate work all day."

Floyd made a face as he carried his weights back over to the rack, then wiped down the bench. "Delicate work?"

"It's a compliment given your career," Greyson laughed. He led Floyd toward the men's locker rooms. "What's your post-workout routine?"

"I don't have one," Floyd admitted.

Greyson nodded. "Scrambled eggs, buttered toast, bacon... treat yourself today," he told him. "Give yourself a good traditional big breakfast. I'll get you more fine-tuned as you go on."

"Oh God, I've done it now. You're never gonna let me go, are you?" Floyd laughed.

"Nope," Greyson agreed with a cheery smile. "When are you working?"

"I'm running the shop all day Friday, but maybe a Saturday class..."

"Definitely join my group class. We do the same kind of weight-lifting while we lunge and squat and so on. You'll feel it the next day," Greyson promised. He laughed. "Especially if you don't goddamn breathe."

"I get caught up!" Floyd insisted. He shoved Greyson's shoulder, and Greyson automatically shoved him back. "This was fun, though." He hadn't done anything this fun in ages. They halted in front of the locker room.

"I gotta get going to set up for a class," Greyson told him, smiling lightly. "But thanks for coming, man."

"No problem. Thanks for the free training. I'll be back," Floyd promised. He took a quick glance around – nobody.

Greyson grabbed his shoulder and leaned in for a quick kiss, their lips warm and tender for just that moment. Then he looked flustered as he pulled back abruptly.

"Bye," Floyd grinned. He kept his voice low and intimate,

for Greyson's ears only. "Can't wait to go up and down with you again."

This time, Greyson turned red. He cleared his throat, raising his hand for a quick wave. "See you." He strode off toward the front desk while Floyd grinned after him.

Floyd's chest was light as he pushed the locker room door open to grab a shower and change. He could get used to this.

Twenty~Three

GREYSON

"Welcome! Come on in!" Jackson beamed as he pushed the screen door open for Greyson, letting him into the house.

"Thanks," Greyson smiled broadly, shaking Jackson's hand and clapping his shoulder in a quick greeting. "I almost forgot about the barbecue," he admitted after a moment, laughing. "A lot happened this week."

"Glad we didn't have to come hunt you down," Cam told him from the background, where he was chopping lettuce.

"Like what?" Jackson added.

In answer, Greyson unbuttoned his shirt sleeve and gently rolled it up to show off the healing sleeve across his forearm. As always, he kept his wrist turned in.

"Oh, shit!" Jackson exclaimed, then grinned. "Guys, come look. This is cool..."

"That's Floyd's work, isn't it?" Chase commented as he pushed himself off the couch to come see. "Yeah, definitely is."

"Nicely spotted," Greyson chuckled. "Can you recognize his work just from--"

Chase was already nodding hard.

"Stupid question, huh?" Greyson laughed.

Chase hedged with a shrug. "Uh... Well, we all have our own styles, that's all."

Greyson grinned. "Right." He pushed his sleeve further up to show off all the way up to his elbow. "It's only at the very beginning stages. We're going to have a couple months of weekly sessions to get the damn things done."

Chase's eyes widened. "Weekly?" He seemed to be trying to find a polite way to ask if Floyd was reckless or not.

"I heal really fast," Greyson added to reassure him.

Chase relaxed and laughed. "Okay. Just making sure."

"That I'm not one of those trouble customers who demands to be healed while I'm scabbing over and gross?"

"Ewww. Not before supper," Thomas complained. "Guys, someone grab the burgers."

"Oh, shit." Jackson took off running for the back door while everyone burst out laughing.

Greyson laughed, too. "Hopefully we don't have burned burgers."

"Nah," Cameron smiled. "They just might not be as juicy as usual."

"Ooooh," Noah smirked, sidling past Cameron to get to the microwave. "That's a shame. The juicier, the better."

Greyson felt at home already, his shoulders sinking with relief at how easily everyone welcomed him in. He hadn't been sure at first if the brothers and their boyfriends would be too insular to really talk to, but they all seemed genuinely pleased to have him around.

God, to have a family like this.

"So Floyd isn't around?"

Alex, who'd been quiet until now as he leaned against the counter and watched the rest of them, spoke up. "Not right now. I think he's at work, right, Chase?"

"Yep. But he spoke very highly of you," Chase said, smirking unmistakably. "So we wanted to invite you around."

Greyson was hard to embarrass, but the way Chase grinned at him made his cheeks feel hot instantly. Everyone *definitely* knew what was up by now, and if they didn't, they guessed. Greyson just didn't know how much Floyd wanted to tell others yet, so... he couldn't really answer that one. "Thanks."

They settled down for supper, and Greyson was relieved that Cam brought up sports instead of his relationship with Floyd as the first topic of conversation. As they grabbed corn cobs, roasted veggies, salad, and burgers, they started bantering about Kevin's chances. From what Greyson knew, Kevin was a good buddy of Floyd's.

"I think he's going to be drafted fast," Cam said with a confident nod. "Great player. He has very good intuition and... well, chemistry. He can read plays and fuckin' read minds sometimes, I swear."

"Yep," Noah laughed. "I don't know the technical terms for it, but he works well as a team with people."

"That's what they wanna see in the pro leagues," Cam said, buttering his corn cob. "You can only get away with being a breakout diva in high school or if your name sounds like a town in Nova Scotia."

Greyson furrowed his brows for a moment, then laughed. "Right. So he's got a good chance, then."

"Yeah. Man, it's weird not having him around," Noah

sighed. He was already half-done his burger – and luckily, the burgers *were* still juicy. "And without Cam..."

"Still not playing, then?" All Greyson knew was that Cam had been out for medical reasons, but he'd gotten fixed up since then. "Are you ever going to?"

Jackson tensed up while Thomas cleared his throat, and Greyson's cheeks flushed with his ignorance. Of course it might be a touchy subject.

Cam didn't seem to mind, though. He still had the same easygoing smile as he nodded. "This summer, starting in my backyard. Still a little nervous of competition."

"Of course," Greyson instantly responded, still feeling guilty for bringing that up over a nice supper. "Yeah... speaking of high school... I just got an email asking if I can donate something for a prize basket for the reunion." He made a face.

Jackson snorted. "That's our good old high school. Bet the organizing committee paid themselves, though."

"Now, you can't assume that," Cam laughed.

"The guys and girls in Greyson's year? Jesus, do you remember them?"

"I do," Alex laughed. "Speaking of divas."

Greyson laughed. That was about damn right. The competition for prom king and queen had been the fiercest of any of the years he'd been in high school, ending with one girl "falling" down a staircase. The prom committee had awarded her the prom queen title, backfiring on the girl everyone suspected had orchestrated it. Violent divas, then. Greyson's brief amusement faded.

Just hearing Noah's lisp or seeing Thomas sway his way around the room was enough to remind Greyson of the young guy he'd once been. He'd had to man up fast between middle and high school, but the same crowd had still remembered the old him no matter how much muscle he'd put on.

He could look after himself now, and he'd been a little luckier in high school, but he was gonna run into a shitload of people with convenient memory loss about middle school.

"I wonder if any of the teachers will show up," Jackson hummed. "I really hated that physics teacher. Mr. Sprouse."

"Oh, fuck. Him," Greyson groaned. "He was so boring."

"I'm so glad he didn't do chemistry."

"The chemistry teacher was awesome." Greyson's memory wasn't yielding a name, but he shook his head. "Exploding shit was great."

They quickly got sucked into a conversation about teachers, since most of them had been the same between Greyson and Jackson's years, and even Cam and Thomas's.

After supper ended, conversation turned to politics, then back to sports and even art. It was hours before Greyson remembered to look at the time.

"Oh my God, it's already nearly my bedtime."

"Your bedtime?" Chase exclaimed. "Boring. God, it's not even nine."

"*Some* of us get up and work out in the morning," Greyson laughed.

Chase smirked and looked over at Jackson, scooting closer to him. "Yeah, some of us do..."

"Too much information," Cam groaned, rising to his feet to see Greyson out.

After they said their goodbyes, Greyson was shocked at how much he couldn't stop smiling. It was so damn easy to spend time around them, and it didn't even feel like they were going out of their way to accommodate him.

Did Floyd get along with them all so well? Presumably, if

he was friends with Kevin and Chase. How big was their damn circle of friends? Certainly bigger than Greyson's, so he was grateful to be welcomed into it so easily.

His cheeks flushed as he walked down the sidewalk toward his own home. More importantly, he couldn't help but wonder what Floyd had said about him to make them want to invite him over.

Maybe he'd ask tomorrow. The thought of seeing Floyd tomorrow made Greyson's smile widen even more.

I'm so stuck on him.

He hummed under his breath as he walked through the quiet evening. Floyd's gorgeous face was all he could see in his mind's eye.

Twenty~Four

FLOYD

The shop door jangled, and before it had even closed, Floyd knew who it was.

Oh, God.

"Ah, Floyd! Hello," Floyd's mother greeted him. It was around noon on Friday, so Floyd hadn't missed any local events... Was she just in the area and wanting to chat?

Somehow, he suspected not.

"Hi, Mom," Floyd answered anyway with a smile. Chase was on the other end of the counter and quickly looked up and over, no doubt eager to see his interactions with his mom. Floyd hoped he wouldn't see the worst of them.

"What are your plans for the weekend?"

And there's the catch. "I have a--"

"I need you to help serve at the church supper," she informed Floyd, folding her hands in front of her as she approached the counter. She always refused to touch anything in here, like she thought she'd contaminate the place – or like it would give her something.

Floyd bit back his annoyance, noticing Chase's raised eyebrow from his peripheral vision. "Oh, that's a shame. I need a few days' notice, Mom." *Like I've always told you.* "I'm going to be working this weekend, or else I could do it."

She frowned for a few moments, then looked over at Chase. "Oh, hello! I don't believe we've met before. You must be the new one, the... Chase?"

"Yes, ma'am," Chase responded with an easygoing smile. He flipped his hair and touched it as she approached, then reached out a hand to shake.

She didn't shake hands, just folded her hands a little closer to herself as she eyed him. "Lovely to meet you. You're as cute as a button. I love your tattoo designs... How long have you been in training?"

Floyd rolled his eyes as she fawned over him. He was used to that guilting technique too, though he almost laughed at how conflicted Chase looked now. He indulged her, talking briefly about his Ontarian training and then how long he'd been here.

When she swept out at last, Chase waited until she was out of view before slowly turning his head to look at Floyd.

"You can say *what the fuck?* if you want," Floyd told him. "I do a lot when I'm done talking to her."

"Okay, then... what the fuck was that?" Chase exclaimed, leaning sideways against the counter to watch Floyd now. "I never... is that normal for her?" He didn't seem to know exactly what to say, but he felt passionate about whatever it was.

Floyd grimaced and looked away, automatically grabbing a rag to wipe the display cabinets. "Um... yeah, pretty much."

"Dude." Chase's voice was quieter now. "Was she trying to

make nice with me to make you feel like a worse son or something?"

This much psychoanalysis was a bit heavy for noon on a Friday. Floyd flinched, then tried to control his instinctive reactions to the blunt truth. He nodded. "Probably."

"You never told me." Chase fidgeted. "And your dad...?"

"He doesn't really talk to me much. Or anyone. He's very introverted," Floyd said slowly, keeping an eye on the front door. "She sort of runs over everyone in her path."

Chase's hand was on his shoulder now, and Floyd resisted the urge to shrug it off. "Why didn't you tell me, then? You know I know all about fucked-up families."

"Yeah, no, that's just it." Floyd glanced at Chase again, his stomach twisting at the memory of the guy's face all winter, while he'd been stressing about his uber-Christian family coming to find him. "You're so much worse off. I don't have a right to complain." Chase was already looking at him like he was an idiot, and Floyd laughed sheepishly.

"Talk to me. That's what friends are for," Chase said in a tone that was firm enough to not leave any doubts in Floyd's mind. "And what about Kevin? Did you talk to him either?"

"No," Floyd admitted. "It's not like anyone can do anything."

"He could come kick her ass. Oh, sorry--" Chase started to apologize, clearly worried he'd crossed a line.

Floyd laughed under his breath and shook his head. "It's fine, man. Just not much to be said about it. It is what it is."

Chase dropped his hand from his shoulder and watched Floyd for a moment or two, but Floyd was determined he was done. There was no sense whining about it when other people had much worse families and they still got on with everyday life. Chase, for example. Floyd admired him a lot more than he'd ever say.

"Okay," Chase concluded after a few moments, then lightly punched his shoulder. "So, Greyson's coming for you... presumably not for the first time...?" He wriggled his eyebrows.

Floyd was absolutely blushing now as he punched Chase's shoulder back, but harder. "Fucking perv."

Chase laughed, staying against the counter while Floyd went to sweep up the front floor. "I'll watch the front tonight while you work on him. Take as long as you need..." he winked.

"We're not banging in the shop."

"Mmhmm."

Floyd couldn't even meet Chase's eyes now, but he kept bursting into laughter anyway. "God, you're a dick."

"I can be," Chase agreed. "I bet he can--"

"Don't," Floyd mock-groaned, brandishing his broom at Chase until Chase held up his hands. "I don't know what... what's going on with us yet."

"Whatever it is, you look good." Chase shrugged. "Okay, I'm grabbing lunch. Be back in a few."

Floyd was a bit relieved for the moment of peace and quiet, his cheeks still hot. What *was* this thing between him and Greyson, anyway?

Whatever it was, he couldn't wait to see him that night.

"Turn your arm over for me. That's it." Floyd smoothed his thumb over the skin he was about to work on, envisioning his next lines, then got to work.

Greyson was a delight to tattoo, and not just because Floyd was so damn stuck on him. Greyson's skin was so nice and smooth on this side, contrasting the scarred ridges on the insides of his arms. Either way, he held the ink really well, and he healed so damn fast. And he held still, and he didn't flinch away and screw up the lines.

"So you were saying about the reunion?" Greyson prompted.

Floyd hummed. "Oh, yeah. I'm not looking forward to being the sad single gay guy still stuck in his hometown..."

"Fuck, you're so much more than that."

Floyd was taken aback by the vehemence of Greyson's tone, lifting the machine for a moment as his eyes flickered up to Greyson's. Then he smiled and got back to work, trying not to waste a moment. The evening was drawing on, and this tattoo wouldn't do itself. "Thanks."

"No, man, I mean it," Greyson murmured. "You own a business now. A lot of people dream of that. And you're damn good at what you do. Your personal life is none of their business."

There was something raw about his voice, and Floyd wondered about it. Greyson hadn't exactly had an easy time through school.

"Well, you're in the same boat, right? Or are you not going to be out to them?" Floyd asked, trying to keep his tone neutral. He couldn't blame Greyson; he'd spent high school dressing, talking, walking manlier. They hadn't really talked back then, but Floyd remembered a softer, quieter, sweeter Greyson.

Before everyone else had gotten their claws in him.

Floyd grimaced, his eyes drawn back to the scars as he worked his way around the side of Greyson's arm.

"I think I will be," Greyson hummed. "Nothing to lose now, right?"

"Right." Floyd half-smiled, trying to pretend this was the first time the idea had occurred to him. "Hey, we should be fake boyfriends for each other. You know, how people arrange for dates for their reunions so they don't look desperate..."

Greyson laughed loudly, the sound ringing. "That's the most romantic proposal I've ever heard."

"Would you take me up on it if I offered seriously?" Floyd raised his eyebrows. He paused his work again to make Greyson meet his eyes.

Greyson hesitated, swallowing hard, then shook his head. It was a jerky motion – not an answer to Floyd's question, but a dismissal of some thought of his own. "We can be fake boyfriends, sure. What the hell."

"These won't be done in time, though, unless..." Floyd trailed off.

Greyson's eyes were lit up with hope now as he tried not to twist toward Floyd, clearly hanging onto his every word.

"You want them to be?"

"At least the insides." Greyson left it unspoken why, but he didn't have to say it. Floyd wasn't stupid.

"Then I'll get the rest of it to match it. Reunion's only a couple weeks away now."

"Yeah." Greyson bit his lip.

Floyd set down the machine for a moment, counting on his fingers as he examined Greyson's arm. "Okay. So, you heal pretty fast, but I can't space them closer together. A week is already pushing it pretty hard."

Greyson nodded slowly.

"But we could do back-to-back sessions. Friday evenings

and Saturday mornings. That shouldn't be too long. I couldn't make it any further apart, though. Since you heal fast, Saturday afternoon or evening you'd already be healing too much. It has to be last thing at night, first thing in the morning. Starting tomorrow, yeah?"

Greyson was nodding again, a grin on his face. "Yeah. You wouldn't mind?"

Of course not. More time spent with you? I'd kill for that. "Fine by me," Floyd nodded. "If I'm taking a guy to my reunion, he'd better look great on my arm."

Greyson settled back as Floyd got back to work. "I thought you were on my arm."

"I think the smaller one takes the bigger one's arm," Floyd frowned.

"Smaller in what way? Because--"

It was a credit to Floyd's training that he kept his hands steady as he flinched and laughed. "Greyson! Christ, don't distract me."

"Is thinking of my cock that distracting?"

Floyd's skin had already been prickling with pleasure at getting to touch and maul Greyson while tattooing him. Yeah, the thought of Greyson's cock was almost enough to get him hard after all that. "Fuck off," he mumbled, focusing on the next swooping line while Greyson's deep chuckle echoed in his ears. "It'll be painful, though," Floyd murmured.

Greyson's eyes widened. "My co--"

"The tattoos!" Floyd exclaimed, laughing again. "The back-to-back sessions. Get your mind out of the gutter."

"Sorry," Greyson winked. "But no, that's fine. I'm just... thanks for doing this for me."

It was said casually, but Floyd could tell Greyson meant

it. He just offered a quick smile. "No problem. Well, there won't be a problem if you shut up about your cock."

Greyson was clearly biting back a comment, and Floyd grinned. "Oh, this is gonna make for some long weekends together."

Not that he resented a single moment.

Twenty~Five

GREYSON

"Lie back and take a couple minutes."

Greyson was happy to listen to Floyd's instructions. His arms itched fiercely with the strange sparks of pain and a dull ache like he'd been working out a little too much. It was all along the surface of his skin, though, rather than localized to a specific muscle.

And he hated to admit it, but despite being – no, *because* he was almost woozy with pain from the marathon session... He felt incredible.

It wasn't the swift, brutal, slicing pain that wrenched emotion out of numbness, but the kind of itching pain that kept him grounded, his thoughts never drifting backward to places he didn't want them to go.

It would be so fucking weird to tell him. Greyson resisted the urge to pick at the bandages over his arms. "Do people get off on this kind of thing?"

"Oh, yeah. Tattooing is a kink," Floyd easily answered as he mopped down the floor. He half-grinned. "A lot of people don't mind it as much as they say. It's only awkward with guys, though."

Greyson laughed, his shoulders settling. The easy reassurance helped him feel a little more normal. But it was the strangest knowledge, knowing that he might never feel that burn of grounding pain across his forearms again. After all, if he did it after the tattoos were done, wouldn't the ink spill out? Or if it healed, it would leave patches across the tattoos. That was the point of this: to keep himself from relapsing.

He wasn't even sure if ink could spill out like that, but he was too wary of Googling it. If it wasn't true... well, the tattoo would be pointless.

He was so wrapped up in thought that he barely noticed Floyd heading for the door. He shook himself out of the moment to stand up, making sure he had his balance and all was fine.

"Can I take you home? We'll settle up the bill tomorrow."

The shop had closed while they were in the back room, and Chase was long gone.

Greyson smiled, stepping out from the hallway back into the main shop. "Sure." He wouldn't complain about getting laid, even if it was brief. He stepped out of the shop, too, to let Floyd activate the alarms.

Floyd joined him on the sidewalk and locked the front door, then took him by the hand.

Greyson squeezed Floyd's hand idly, then set off walking. He fully expected to invite Floyd inside and have him over – maybe even overnight this time.

They didn't say much along the way; after hours together in that little brightly-lit room, they'd said it all already. Greyson was sure Floyd's brain and hands hurt from the concentration, but he hadn't breathed a word of complaint.

"Here we go," Floyd murmured as they reached Greyson's door. He came to a halt and Greyson let go of his hand to unlock the door. When he pushed it open, Floyd didn't move to follow him.

Greyson gave him a questioning glance.

"Good night, then," Floyd nodded with a light smile, reaching out to pull Greyson back toward him.

Oh, he doesn't want to...? Greyson hesitated, then let Floyd pull him back onto the porch. He sidled up closer to him, sliding his arms gingerly around Floyd's waist and leaning in for a gentle kiss.

It was tender more than anything, Floyd's eyelids heavy with sleep. Greyson's anxieties settled instantly; it wasn't Floyd getting freaked out by the scars or anything. He was just tired out.

"You good for tomorrow?" Greyson pulled back enough to murmur against Floyd's soft, sweet lips.

"I'm fine for tomorrow," Floyd confirmed, smiling lightly at him. He leaned in to peck his lips again, his body warm and solid against Greyson's.

Greyson finally backed up again, his arms sliding away, then touched Floyd's arm. "Thanks for tonight."

"Thank *you*."

Floyd turned and headed down the porch stairs, then waved and said good night as Greyson headed inside.

"Good night." Greyson closed the door after a few lingering moments of watching Floyd walk off down to the sidewalk. Then, he leaned against it and let a smile cross his face.

He'd *wanted* Floyd to stay overnight. That meant a lot more than he could explain.

It felt a bit like every time he blinked, Greyson was back with Floyd again. Maybe that was exhaustion talking from the late night last night, then the early morning.

He was back in the tattoo chair, and though *he'd* been the one up at six for a jog, Floyd looked far more awake than he did.

Greyson had figured he'd take ages to fall asleep with Floyd on his mind last night, but he'd wound up conking out like a light. He'd forgotten how much pain – even manageable, slight pain – tired him out. There'd been a day it was the only way he could get some sleep.

But it was a bright morning, and Greyson was able to put that out of his head easily enough.

"I need some of whatever coffee you've got," Greyson smiled.

Floyd laughed, his eyes too focused still on Greyson's bicep as he outlined more tracing curls. "On the next break, I'll give you some."

"How was your night, then? I assume you slept well from the spring in your step," Greyson complained.

"You're usually the morning person," Floyd smirked. "Did I keep you out past your bedtime?"

Greyson's cheeks were hot as he laughed. "Maybe."

"Really?"

"Shut up," Greyson lamented. "I like having a normal sleep schedule these days. Even if it's early." It made a great change from his old life, where he'd been up at all hours from week to week.

"But my night was good," Floyd answered, smiling simply. "Had a dream about an animated meadow coming to life."

"That's very artistic." Greyson searched his memory for dreams. "I don't remember much of mine. I was too tired out." He cleared his throat, glancing up at Floyd for a moment. "You don't mind seeing me twice in twenty-four hours?"

Floyd lifted the needle so he could pointedly roll his eyes. "If I minded, I wouldn't have suggested it. Stop your worrying."

"Right." Greyson felt sheepish as he laughed. "But our date tomorrow...?"

"That better still be on," Floyd threatened idly and laughed. "Or I'm going to be upset, and upset tattoo artists--"

"Yeah, it's on," Greyson quickly grinned. They shared a smile for a moment, and then Floyd got back to it, pinpricks of pain racing their way down his bicep.

"So we're basically spending the weekend together. And if you come to class today – which you should – it'll be the whole damn weekend," Greyson laughed.

Floyd hummed. "I don't know if I can keep up with the others. How fit is this class?"

"God." Greyson flipped his arm for Floyd when he asked him to. "Now you're gonna get all insecure? People of all skill levels come to classes. Everything is adapted person by person." Floyd had seemed so tentative lifting weights, like he was worried about his own strength.

In general, Floyd seemed to have trouble owning his strength. Greyson frowned at the thought.

"Right," Floyd nodded quickly. "Okay, fine, I'll come to class."

Greyson smirked. "Good."

Minutes ticked into hours until lunchtime, when they headed down to the cafe for sandwiches and coffee. Then they got back to it, working until Floyd told Greyson he literally couldn't do another minute.

"Jesus, you did more than enough," Greyson told Floyd to cut off any apologies. "That was, what, eight hours? It's been all fuckin' day!"

"Yeah," Floyd laughed quietly. "I don't do marathon sessions for just everyone."

They caught each other's eyes while Floyd disassembled the tattoo gun by touch alone. It was a quiet moment of acknowledgment.

"But I owe you for the gym training--"

"Nooo," Greyson groaned. "Oh, God, no, don't do that."

"I'm doing it." Floyd grinned stubbornly. "We're trading, like it or not."

"I want to pay you."

"I don't want you to pay me."

Greyson patted down his pockets. "Let me pay you."

"I'll bandage your hands, too, if you try."

Greyson stared. "Hey!"

Floyd winked. "Don't think I won't." Once the parts of the machine were in what looked like a sterilizing machine, he approached Greyson to bandage up his arms again, his touch skillful and light.

Even though they'd shared hours of light conversation and hours of silence, the effect Floyd had on him wasn't gone. Greyson's skin felt like it was standing in goosebumps the closer Floyd stood to him, and he couldn't tear his eyes away from Floyd's lips.

"Kiss me, then," Floyd murmured, dropping his voice to a murmur. "Since you can't stop watching me like that."

Greyson instantly obeyed, pushing himself to sit sideways on the tattoo chair with his spread legs on either side of

Floyd's. He gripped Floyd's hands through the protective gloves, lacing their fingers together roughly as he leaned in and kissed Floyd in an open-mouthed promise.

Floyd moaned into his mouth, his spine curving as his shoulders sank and he pushed forward into the human contact. It must have been nice to feel after hours of one-way contact, so Greyson dropped one of Floyd's hands to gently massage the other hand with both of his own.

Floyd moaned his approval, then murmured, "Oh, s'nice."

Finding this little button of pleasure made Greyson's back straighten with pride. He could do this for him after every session, at least. He kept kissing Floyd in gentle, quiet, open-mouthed kisses, keeping himself from pressing any closer to Floyd since he didn't want to wind up fucking in the workplace. A minute or two later, he switched to rubbing the other hand until his own hands started to cramp.

"Okay," Floyd finally murmured with a breathy laugh. "I'll come to the gym for class tonight. Scram, I gotta clean up."

Greyson grinned and pushed himself to his feet, then leaned over Floyd's stool and braced his hands on each of Floyd's knees for one more nice, slow kiss. "See you tonight."

"See you," Floyd murmured, then pushed his chest lightly to get him out of there. He was grinning the whole time, and Greyson's mind felt light with pleasure at the expression.

Floyd was gorgeous when he smiled like that.

CHAPTER
Twenty-Six
FLOYD

"SERIOUSLY?"

Floyd leaned back in his car seat, glaring at his phone. His arms hurt, so he had to rest his phone on the steering wheel to skim the Grindr message he'd just gotten. He was about three seconds away from deleting his profile, and this message hardly helped.

Need a date to the reunion?

The profile that sent the message was blank, but he knew exactly who it was: Brett, the asshole.

"Fuck you and fuck your smarmy little face." Floyd opened the car door and climbed out, heading to his front door while doing his best to ignore the burning pain in all of his limbs, and even through his core.

Greyson hadn't been kidding when he'd promised group classes were a workout. They'd still had a lot of fun and laughter, which Floyd now suspected was a ploy to keep them working harder without noticing the pain for as long.

Oh, God, if this was what it took to get in shape, Floyd was happy to be the out-of-shape one in this relationship.

Not relationship, he reminded himself quickly, his breath catching in his throat. He unlocked the door to let himself inside, then gingerly bent to take off his shoes. What he had with Greyson wasn't yet... what he could call a relationship, exactly.

He *had* to ask soon.

It took him a minute to remember why his phone was in his hand. "Oh, right. That asshole."

He opened up the app again and typed out a quick response.

Nope, I've got one :)

Then he put down the phone to drop off his gym clothes in the laundry basket. By the time he got back, the profile was deleted.

Floyd laughed loudly. Considering how nervous Brett had made him the first time, he wasn't taking him at all seriously this time around. What had changed?

Brett would definitely be at the reunion and jealous of Greyson. Even the prospect of facing him didn't faze Floyd right now, though. Maybe it was all the adrenaline from his workout, or the opposite – exhaustion tiring out any anxiety he might have felt. Either way, Floyd was still smiling.

He rolled his shoulders and went to grab supper, his mind racing. Between tattoos this morning and afternoon and the group workout this evening, his arms were about ready to give out. He had to be careful as he grabbed leftovers to reheat.

Floyd was loving riding high on this self-confidence, though. He'd forgotten what a fresh workout felt like and how it left the blood pumping. He'd also forgotten how much it made him want to smack a bastard down, and Brett definitely counted as one. His secret weapon was Greyson pretending to be his boyfriend, since he knew Brett would probably be afraid of facing Greyson again.

It was horrible of him to be pleased about that, since he didn't support what Greyson had done to Brett the first time around – no broken bones, but plenty of bruising. But somehow, Floyd didn't care. He was over worrying about assholes like Brett.

Floyd was much more concerned with thinking about Greyson. Bringing him as his fake boyfriend was nowhere near what he wanted.

"I'm stuck on him."

He had to call Kevin soon. He was off on Monday and Tuesday, so surely he'd have time to talk through this with him.

But what was there to talk through?

It wasn't like he hadn't been through this before. Floyd had dated before – even if he'd chosen the wrong guys. He knew what he wanted this time around, too. He just didn't know if Greyson felt the same.

The lighthouse overlooking the waterfront and river was a gorgeous little spot for a date, especially on a sunny Sunday afternoon. It was even better in good company, and Floyd couldn't think of any better company than Greyson.

Every time he spent time with him, Floyd marveled over how casual it felt. It was like hanging out with a best friend, except... Best friends didn't look at each other like Floyd kept watching Greyson. He was so fucking *cute*, strong, and smart. He was the whole damn package.

Floyd even let him order a cider for him. And then several more.

"You been to the bar on the other side of the river yet?"

"Not yet," Floyd admitted with a smile. Bars weren't good places for him, in general. He'd heard about it opening, but he hadn't been. "Why?"

"We could walk over there, check it out," Greyson offered, then nodded at the glass. "Once we're done these, obviously."

"And have *more* drinks?"

Greyson laughed. "Yeah, maybe. Why not?"

"I'm gonna be falling into your bed tonight," Floyd winked. He was already pleasantly buzzed, his skin tingling.

Greyson shook his head, leaning back as he smiled at Floyd. "Nah, not tonight, on either count. Maybe soon though, hm?"

"That's... very decent of you," Floyd stuck out his lower lip as he nodded his appreciation.

Greyson laughed again. "Anyway, where was I?"

"Alberta."

"Right! When I got my first patrol there, the – the dog park incident."

Floyd leaned back with his cider, his eyes fixed on Greyson's face. He kept missing bits of his story, too fascinated by watching the way Greyson's expressions shifted as he gestured and beamed. "Uh huh," he nodded when he noticed Greyson waiting for responses.

Greyson finished his story and his cider, and Floyd laughed when he ordered one more for each of them.

Being a little tipsy, talking about stupid shit, sharing bits of their lives... He hadn't done this for years, and somehow, he liked it.

"You gonna manage?"

"I'm not drunk yet," Floyd laughed. Far from it; though his tolerance was lower than it had been years ago, he was still a big guy, and they'd been drinking slowly as they caught up on their lives. "God. I might not be ripped, but that's just insulting."

Greyson laughed loudly. "Sorry," he apologized, then started the last drink with Floyd, reaching out to clink their glasses together.

"I haven't had this much to drink in years, though," Floyd told him, his smile fading slightly. "Other than that time with you. It... I had a bit of a problem. After... you know... things happened."

Greyson was watching him seriously now, sipping his drink and letting him continue at his own pace.

"It was pretty hard on everyone around me. But I got better, and... yeah, I don't drink on my own much anymore," Floyd laughed under his breath. That was the most he wanted to say about it anyway.

"Good for you," Greyson nodded simply.

"I don't usually like who I am when I'm drunk, but it's different around you." *Maybe I **am** a little more tipsy than usual.* Floyd bit his tongue, resolving not to say anything more.

Greyson grinned again, reaching out to clap his arm. "That's because I'm so awesome."

"Maybe we can do this more often. Like... a lot more often. Not *this* this," Floyd hastened to add while Greyson laughed at him. "I mean, in general."

"Are you asking me out?"

Floyd hesitated, taking a breath to clear his head. His fingers tingled where he wrapped them around the cold glass, and he rubbed lines through the condensation as he thought about his answer. *Damn it, I shouldn't have said more.* "Um... I want to. What do you think?"

Greyson blew out a quiet sigh. He didn't seem put-upon – just nervous, which was always amusing and adorable on him. He didn't tend to get scared easily, which was something Floyd had always admired about him. Of course, it also made him more likely to walk straight into the face of danger, but it got him out, too.

"I don't know," Greyson admitted honestly. "I have a lot on the go, too, and... I don't think I can be a very good boyfriend. Yet."

Floyd nodded slowly, biting back his disappointment.

"Fake boyfriend, for sure," Greyson teased to lighten the mood. Floyd let him do it and smiled in return. "You can try before you buy. And dates... I like dates."

"And tattoos, and fitness classes?" Floyd grinned.

Greyson didn't even pause a second to think about it. "Yeah."

"I'm okay with that," Floyd nodded. "So we're dating, we're just not... *dating.*"

"Yeah," Greyson nodded slowly. He reached across the table to run his fingers along the tips of Floyd's, over the cool glass. The contrast in heat and cold made Floyd shiver, but he tried to let go of his desire. They definitely weren't hooking up drunk with what Greyson had said earlier.

Instead, Floyd let go of his glass and turned his hand palm-up on the table to let Greyson touch his palm and fingers.

"Brr," Greyson teased. "Did they chill yours down to freezing? God. Mine's only half that cold." He turned his palm face-up, and Floyd played along, running his fingers down across the callused palms and fingers. They laced fingers with each other for a moment, eyes locked.

Greyson's eyes were warm, and though his expression was still nervous, he had a smile on his face he couldn't seem to wipe away.

Floyd felt just the same.

"We should get going, then," Floyd finally said, pulling away from Greyson's touch to finish his cider before he rose to his feet.

As natural as breathing, Greyson's hand slipped into Floyd's when they walked down the sidewalk from the restaurant toward their houses.

When it was time for them to part ways, Greyson's house a few minutes' walk in one direction while Floyd's apartment building was several minutes the other, they both paused on the sidewalk and turned to each other.

"I'm really glad you told me that," Greyson said quietly, and Floyd didn't have to ask what he meant. "Thank you."

"Thank you for bringing up the dating thing," Floyd countered. "We'll... talk more about it as things go on, eh?"

"Yeah."

Floyd made himself let go of Greyson's hand at last. He leaned in, cupping Greyson's cheek for a nice, sweet goodbye kiss before they waved and went on their separate ways.

It was easy to fall into Greyson's company, but it was getting harder each time for Floyd to tear himself away.

Twenty-Seven

KEVIN

IT WAS WEIRD NOT TO BE WAITING AT THE BAGGAGE CLAIM FOR his stick. With just his backpack, Kevin walked straight out of the arrivals gate, glancing around for Cam.

"Hey, ugly mug."

Kevin laughed and spotted Cam instantly with the verbal cue, a head above the others he was standing near. "Gee, thanks." He strode up to Cam for a tight, back-slapping hug, then pulled back. "Long time no see, huh?"

"Only a month," Cam grinned. "Wait 'til game season starts. You'll be up and down the goddamn continent more than... well." He couldn't finish that metaphor in public.

Kevin laughed and let go of Cam, then punched his arm. "You're looking great."

"You, too, though. Considering. You're bulking up, too," Cam complimented, looking him up and down. "Trainer got you working out more?"

Kevin groaned. He didn't even have to tell Cam, who used to get coached by the same guy, what the man put them all through. He was demanding, but in a good way – the kind of guy who wanted you to be your best.

"Come on, I'm parked over here."

As they walked, Kevin elbowed Cam. "So, things are going good?"

"Great," Cam nodded. "Noah's... well. Noah's good." The way he glowed when he talked about his boyfriend was sweet, even if it made Kevin's heart hurt a little with jealousy.

"That's informative. Thanks."

"You're welcome." Cam gave him an obnoxious grin, then sobered up a little. "You wanted to come check on Floyd?"

"Yeah, he's... He's been weird lately, even over the phone." But this was more than helping Floyd out. Kevin needed a break himself from the intensity of... well... everything. Kevin didn't care if he spent his precious break mostly on planes, as long as he got to see his friends and family again for a bit. Even for half a day each.

"He has," Cam agreed with a nod. "I think he's in love."

Kevin stopped dead, his hand on the car handle. "What?"

"He hasn't told you?"

"He's been really cagey," Kevin frowned, then climbed in as Cam did. How come he'd told Cam and not him? Was something wrong? God, he hoped Floyd wasn't crushing on him or something.

Cam nodded. "He has been with us, too, but he's been mentioning a lot about this guy, a former friend of his. We had him over for a barbecue and he seems really cool, though."

"What's the guy's name?"

"Greyson."

Kevin recognized it, but he couldn't place it exactly.

Maybe from school. "Okay, cool. Wow. That's a lot better than I was worrying about."

"Why, what were you worried about?"

"His parents are... well. Pretty weird." Kevin wasn't sure how much he should say, but that much at least seemed safe.

Cam frowned. "Really?"

"For sure. His mom especially."

Cam hummed as he drove through the woods toward town, keeping an eye out for wild animals. "So how's training going? What do they have you doing?"

Kevin was glad to change the subject and talk in detail about hockey instead of Floyd, but he was also painfully aware of Cam's interest in it. His buddy had to be at least a little jealous, even if he hid it well. A sudden medical condition taking him out was any guy's worst nightmare, let alone one who was just about to get the contract of his life.

As they reached the outskirts of town, marked by a huge bridge passing overhead, Kevin glanced at Cam again. "Is Floyd working today?"

"I asked Chase and he didn't think so. Why?"

"We could drop by and surprise him." Cam was probably Kevin's other closest friend, so they could stage an intervention if they had to.

Cam laughed. "That'll be a hell of a surprise, but sure. Did you tell him at all you were coming out?"

"Nope," Kevin grinned.

When they pulled up in front of Floyd's apartment, Kevin left his backpack in the car and headed up to the door, squinting at the buzzers until he found Floyd's.

"Hello?"

"Hey, man," Cam spoke up. "It's Cam. You in? Now a good time to drop by?"

"Oh yeah, yeah. Come on in."

The buzzer rang off and the door clicked open.

Kevin grinned at Cam and pulled open the door, waiting for the elevator with him. "Nicely done."

"Thanks."

They headed up in the elevator. By the time the elevator door opened, Floyd had his apartment door open and was leaning in the frame. "Hey, Ca–holy shit! Kev?"

"Hey, man," Kevin beamed at Floyd, striding forward for a quick, tight hug and slapping him on his back. "They gave us two days off, so I'm here 'til tomorrow morning."

"Oh my God, man, you could've told me!" Floyd laughed. He slapped Kevin's back and then held his door open for both Cam and Kevin to get in, clapping Cam's arm as well.

"Nah, I wanted to surprise you."

"Well, you did," Floyd laughed. Floyd's face was a little more taut, like he was wound up about something but trying to put it aside for the sake of the visit.

Kevin nodded. "How have you been? You're cagey as shit on the phone. Be real."

Floyd opened his mouth, then closed it again and nodded slowly. He seemed uncertain about exactly what to say, but he let out a quiet breath. "Basically... there's this guy."

"Oho," Kevin clapped his hands together and leaned forward. "I knew it."

Floyd groaned. "Fuck off. Anyway, he has... his own kind of problems."

"Like all of us," Cam supplied.

Floyd conceded that one with a shrug. "Yeah. But it's making him think he wouldn't be a good boyfriend."

He wants to date the guy? Holy shit. Kevin grinned. "On the good news, he wants to be your boyfriend other than that, huh?"

Floyd flopped on the couch, and Cam and Kevin followed suit, flanking him. "Yeah, I think," Floyd admitted.

"So what's the problem? You think he's not committed?" Cam asked, leaning back and folding his arms.

"You guys want a pop or something?" Floyd offered, but Kevin grabbed his shoulder.

"Sure, but hold on, hold on. Don't run so fast," Kevin laughed. "I know that face." Floyd always had a certain look when he was trying to escape a tricky conversation.

Floyd grimaced but stayed sitting down. "Fine. Yeah. I just think he feels like he has to be perfect. He's really... hard on himself."

"So have you told him you like him the way he is? Or love him?" Kevin asked, watching Floyd closely.

Floyd caught his breath, but the moment of stunned silence said it all.

"You do," Kevin murmured, raising his brows. "Jesus. That's fast."

Floyd heaved himself to his feet to go grab pop, his hands fidgeting anxiously. Kevin didn't follow, just cast a quick glance at Cam and stayed where he was to give him a bit of space. "Yeah, I know," Floyd told them from the kitchen.

"So have you told him? Either of those things?"

Floyd shook his head, handing over a can of pop to each of them and cracking his own as he sank down onto the coffee table, sitting facing them both. "Not yet." He took the first sip carefully.

Cam nodded. "So just fuckin' tell him."

"But--" Floyd started.

"He's going to argue it," Kevin laughed, kicking Floyd's

knee lightly as he looked at Cam. "Not everyone is blunt. And I seem to remember *you* didn't tell Noah everything--"

"Shut up," Cam groaned. "Point is, get it out now. I wish I'd said more, earlier."

Floyd frowned. He was taking Cam's advice, but something still bothered him. "And if he just thinks I'm a fling? We have to spend a lot of time together over the next few weeks..."

"Suck it up, princess," Cam snorted. "Put up or shut up."

Kevin heard Coach Walker in his voice and laughed.

Floyd joined in the laugh a moment later and shook his head as he sipped. "Yeah. Guess you're right, huh? Anyway – what the fuck are *you* doing here?" he addressed Kevin, relaxing and grinning at him.

Kevin rolled his eyes. "I got a couple days off for good behavior, and I thought I'd come visit my family and friends like a sentimental asshole."

"Aww, how sweet," Floyd grinned. "If I'd known, we could have done a party tonight. Wait, did you know?"

"Only a couple days ago," Cam shook his head. "I can confirm that it wasn't a premeditated plan," he laughed. "But he's coming over for a couple beers tonight if you wanna come," he offered Floyd.

Kevin glanced at Floyd. From what he knew, he wasn't much for drinking, but he did hope he came just to get a better chance to talk to him.

"I've got supper with my parents..." Floyd trailed off, then frowned. "I can get away early, yeah."

"After supper? I'm having supper with my family, too." Kevin punched Floyd's arm lightly. "Hey, man, about that..." There was no easy way to say it. "You doing all right with them?"

"Oh, yeah, yeah. Yeah... Yeah." Floyd gulped his pop and nodded again.

Cam burst out laughing. "Well, that's convincing."

Floyd's cheeks flushed and he scuffed a foot on the floor in an anxious tic. "Jesus, is it waterboard-Floyd-day today?"

"I'm just saying, man, things seem pretty shitty. If you need anything, bro..." Kevin shook his head. "Man, my mom would be there."

"Or mine," Cam nodded. "She's only met you, like, twice, but she'd trade you for me, I'm sure."

That made Floyd laugh, at least. "Thanks. Yeah, it's... it's nice to be welcomed into the family. It's so easy to be around you guys."

Kevin smiled over at Cam, jerking his chin toward him. "Yeah, I know."

Cam just gave a broad shrug. "Of course. Anyway, finish your pop," he told Kevin, jerking his thumb toward the window. "Speaking of family, I gotta get you to your parents' place. I think they'll wanna see you."

"Awesome." Kevin gulped down the last of the pop, then set aside the can and stood up again. "See you tonight, right?" he addressed Floyd as Floyd stood, too.

"Of course. Tonight, man."

"See you, bro."

Kevin shook his head as he pulled his shoes back on to follow Cam to his car to go see his parents. Floyd was in love, Cam was in love – actually, all the Rileys now... At this rate, there wouldn't be a single guy left in their group except him.

CHAPTER
Twenty~Eight
GREYSON

"Y OU SAID BEFORE THAT YOU MET SOMEONE YOU LIKE — AND now you're seeing them?"

"Him," Greyson corrected, his jaw firm.

Greyson's mother nodded slightly. "We just wanted you to know that we worry about you."

All parents did, but sometimes it didn't feel like Greyson's parents' concern came from anywhere good. At least they were acknowledging his corrections, even if they shouldn't have been needed.

"But you're not in Alberta anymore. Things are a lot slower to change around here," his father spoke up.

Greyson squinted, trying to figure out what that meant. "So...?"

"So... well..." They exchanged looks. "The more sensitive you are, the harder it will be to get past whatever you went through before."

"Are you..." Greyson trailed off. "What?"

"We understand being a police officer is hard," his mother

interrupted. "But refusing to rejoin just because of what happened here last time--"

"Mom." That stopped her, and they both watched him from the couch. Greyson rubbed his forehead as he leaned back in the armchair. They knew he'd been involved in an off-duty incident. He might have implied that it was with a known troublemaker – which it was – and that he'd been targeted because he was a cop. Not that he'd gone to enforce vigilante justice on an asshole who was never going to be picked up by the system.

As always, his mistruths came back to bite him in the ass.

"We just worry that you're drifting back to being... well..."

"Girly?" Greyson raised his eyebrow, folding his arms just to subtly highlight his biceps. He'd recently switched to more upper body training.

"No. Just..."

"The kid who got picked on all through grade school? Yeah, I'm not that guy anymore," Greyson told them. Far from it. It was like they didn't even know him. God knew what image of him they really had.

"No, but life would be a lot easier..."

"Yeah, it would," Greyson agreed with his dad. "Yeah, I know being a fitness instructor is gayer than being a cop. And I know some people will have a problem with me, but I'm more than equipped to handle those guys now. And yeah, I went through... crap... before, in Alberta and here. But I'm not becoming a sensitive little pansy--" *like you're afraid of, Dad,* "--just because I'm dating a man. You have... a lot of... mixed-up ideas."

They considered that for a moment before Greyson's mother nodded. "I suppose we do. We just don't know how to have a..."

"Gay son?"

"Yes."

Greyson half-smiled. "You just listen to me, support me when I bring someone home, stand up for me when your friends say homophobic things, and respect me like you would if I were the 200-pound cop still, dating women and seeming happy."

"But you *are* happier now?" his mother asked, and his father watched him closely. He could tell they weren't sure *how*, exactly, hence the question.

"Duh," Greyson smiled, leaning back again and unfolding his arms. *I mean, technically, I am. I'm a little healthier.* "I'm dealing with all my crap. I just need to... not get unsolicited advice. And no matter how much I miss it, I can't do my old job anymore. It brings up too much for me."

"I just wish we could've protected you better--"

Greyson stood up to sit next to his mother, taking her hand and squeezing it. "Mom. Kids will be kids. You couldn't keep me safe from everyone. But I learned to keep myself safe." And yeah, part of that was squashing down everything until he hummed with the need to feel something, but he'd done what he'd had to then, too.

And now he was dealing with his shit.

"In fact," Greyson spoke up with a light smile to interrupt her guilt, "the guy I'm seeing knows a lot of the past stuff going on with me and he still wants to be around me."

"Good. He wouldn't be worth being around if he didn't," his father said firmly.

Greyson almost flinched from surprise. He hadn't expected that much passion in his dad's voice, let alone using *those* pronouns. "I... yeah."

Yeah, Floyd knew a lot about him, and that made him a

little uncomfortable. But it ensured that he couldn't hide from his issues anymore, and maybe that was healthy.

And Floyd wanted to date him. He'd hinted that at the lighthouse restaurant.

I could date him, if he can put up with me.

Greyson moved to hug his mother, then nodded at his dad. At least they were on his side after all.

AT FIRST, FLOYD DIDN'T REMEMBER WHY HIS HANDS WERE STIFF and his stomach jittered with nerves as he rolled over slowly in bed, stretching.

Then, he yawned, a smile spreading over his face. A marathon session of tattooing left his hands feeling a little sore the next day, but he soaked them in warm water, rubbed lotion in, and they were usually good to go again. Then again, two back-to-back marathons? He'd never done this for any other guy, and he didn't think he'd want to again.

But this was his last tattoo session with Greyson. They'd get it done with a couple weeks before the reunion for the tattoos to properly heal, and then... well, he'd look some hot in his short-sleeved shirt. Whether he was Floyd's boyfriend by then or not.

Yesterday's session had felt so utterly comfortable he hadn't felt the need to bring up their relationship status yet. But now that the work was almost over, he had to. They were two weeks away from the reunion, and the more he thought about it, the more Floyd knew he didn't want to go as *fake* boyfriends.

He had to tell Greyson he didn't care what kind of issues he had going on, he'd date the *fuck* out of him. Or something like that. The good-night kiss had been longer than usual this time, and the way Greyson watched him...

"Tell me I'm not going crazy," Floyd groaned to the empty air of the bedroom, pulling the pillow over his face.

"I don't know if you are--"

"What the *fuck*?" Floyd exclaimed, sitting bolt-upright as he heard a woman's voice from outside the bedroom. Then, not even a second later, he recognized it. "*Mom?!*"

"I don't know why you're lying in when the church lunch preparation has long since started--"

"What?" Floyd threw the covers off, his nerves sparking in anger. "Wait, no." He stepped into jeans and pulled on a t-shirt, brushing his hands vigorously back and forth through his hair a few times to try to tame the bedhead.

Then, he threw open his bedroom door.

His mother stood there, clearly dressed for church. Her brows drew together as she gave a disapproving tut. "That's hardly appropriate. And neither is that language, young man."

"You're--" Floyd was genuinely worried for her mental health now. It was like she was in her own house, not *his* goddamn place. "That's-- stop. Just stop. What are you doing in *my* place? Is this an emergency?"

"Well, I assumed you would be helping this weekend in lieu of last weekend, when you were apparently too busy for me."

"No. *No*. That's not how that works. You never gave me warning last time or even asked me this time," Floyd told her heatedly. It was too early in the morning for him to have his guard up against drama, and he was sick and tired of this shit.

"Oh. So you're going to go your own way again?" She straightened up, shouldering her purse. "Never lifting a finger to help your own family, only concerned with your own selfish interests?"

"My own-- Mom, you literally didn't tell me you wanted me to help this weekend-- no, let me finish! To help this weekend. Then you use my spare key, I'm assuming, since you can't kick a door down in that dress without making a racket. Without my permission. If I'd had my boyfriend--"

"Your *what*?"

Silence ticked by for a few seconds as Floyd stared pointedly at her. Sure, Greyson technically wasn't – *yet*, he tried not to think – but the point was still valid.

"I can't believe you wouldn't tell me this."

Floyd huffed out a sigh of annoyance.

"So this is why you're suddenly so unhelpful. Well, it's better than the booze, I suppose. Marginally." She turned around and marched for the front door, Floyd following close behind to open it for her. "Let me know when you're ready to make good on your promise of doing better."

She doesn't care about me. The realization was a punch to the gut. *She cares about making me do what she wants me to.*

It wasn't like Floyd hadn't known that for years.

But now... something about the stark shift in her attitude made him see it more clearly than ever. She hadn't even paused to ask who it was. She'd instantly pulled out her ultimate weapon – his past – and tried to make it about her.

He was done trying to impress people who didn't care. He'd stopped owing her favors and apologies years ago.

"I'll take the key." She silently pressed it into his hand. "Bye, Mom. I'll call you."

She was out the door in seconds, too deep in one of her self-righteous rage fits to say goodbye as she marched down the apartment hall to the parking lot. Someone was in the driver's seat of her car – presumably his dad.

Floyd glowered at the door lock as if it had personally betrayed him by letting her in this morning, then closed the door hard and leaned on it.

Christ. Not even in his own home was he safe from that woman. And his dad didn't seem to give a damn. He never once spoke up to ask if she was being reasonable, or to defend Floyd. Did they both think he was a good-for-nothing dropout cop on the bottle?

Well... no sense standing about moping. He had a job to do: one of the most important jobs he'd ever done.

Greyson's self-confidence rested on Floyd's shoulders right now, and Floyd was going to do his damnedest to help.

"So, I think we should talk." Floyd leaned over his coffee and sandwich, ignoring the hustle and bustle of the café at lunchtime.

The morning had been as peaceful as yesterday, and setting aside his own grim thoughts for a few hours had been most welcome. They'd both needed a break and lunch before they kept going, though, so they were here again. The baristas were starting to recognize them.

"I agree," Greyson said seriously, putting down the crust of his sandwich and pushing his plate aside. "You go first."

Floyd's anxiety ratcheted up a notch, but he tried to

ignore it. *I need to take the risk that I could hurt him. I **can** hurt people, and I can let them help me with whatever I'm dealing with.* He drew a breath and let it out, then sipped his coffee and cleared his throat.

"I just wanted to say... I know you've got your own stresses, but man, I don't care."

Greyson looked taken aback as he leaned back, his hands wrapped around his cup. "You what?"

"I mean, I *care*," Floyd hastily continued. "Of course. No, I mean... um..." His cheeks flushed as Greyson started to smirk.

That goddamn smirk. There it was again – the cocky bit of him. The bit of him who'd acted like he deserved a thanks for punching Floyd's asshole ex in the face.

He kind of liked that bit.

Floyd rubbed his face. "Stop looking at me like that. I like you, okay? Let's be adults about this. I like you, and I don't care if you're a little screwed-up--"

Greyson flinched but nodded slightly.

"--sorry, but you know what I mean. Cause I am, too. And I've been worried that..." Floyd trailed off, grimacing.

"That what?"

"That I'll hurt you. I keep letting everyone around me down," Floyd told him quietly, warming his hands on his mug to soothe the ache.

"You haven't let me down," Greyson shook his head. "You've come through for me. For my part, I've been holding off telling you because of all this--"

"The tattoo sessions?"

"Yeah. Forty hours of awkwardness--"

"*Right?!*" Floyd exclaimed, his laugh ringing out and startling even himself. Thank God Greyson had been worried about the same stupid little stuff. "All day trying to pretend we're not crazy into each other..."

"We are," Greyson agreed, and Floyd couldn't look away from those enchanting dark eyes. "I have been for... a long time. I think back then, when I stood up for you..."

Floyd's brows shot up. "You crushed on me back *then*?"

Now Greyson looked embarrassed as he set down his cup with a loud *clunk* against the table. "Maybe. Anyway, that's beside the point! Let's get out of here."

"I think it's very relevant," Floyd smirked. He loved cracking through that confident, cool attitude to the embarrassed little nerd Greyson kept so well-hidden. He stood up, following Greyson out into the rainy afternoon.

Before he could set off in a brisk stride just down the street to his shop almost next door, Greyson grabbed his arm to hold him back. "I'm trying to ask you something," Greyson laughed, his cheeks red. "Without other people around."

"Go ahead." Floyd was getting rained on, but Greyson... looked like he had something to say. He paused and turned back to face Greyson.

"Do you want to date? For real?"

Oh, wow. Floyd hadn't expected to hear that from Greyson, and he knew his shock registered easily on his face. "You-- really? What's changed? You really want to?"

Greyson gave him a *duh* look. "No, it's sarcasm. Of course I want to date you. I... thought more about it, that's all."

Floyd laughed. It was his turn for embarrassment again as he stared down for a moment, then shook his head slowly as he looked back up at Greyson, a smile crossing his lips. "I was just worried you were putting up with me until the tattoos were done--"

Greyson stepped forward, grabbing his cheeks and hauling him in for a kiss.

Someone nearby wolf-whistled, and Floyd nearly burst out laughing against Greyson's soft lips. It was *wonderful* to kiss him in the warm summer rain, as much of a fucking stereotype as that was. And they didn't have to damn well hide down alleys to do it. If he wanted to kiss Greyson right here in the middle of the sidewalk, he could do it.

Floyd kissed Greyson back just as hard, his hands rising to grip Greyson's hips. He pulled him in against him, their fronts pressing warmly together as their lips slid against each other's. Floyd's chest burned with warmth at Greyson's impulsive, passionate move.

He loved Greyson's impulsive, passionate side. He didn't love the trouble it got him into sometimes, but Christ, he could deal with that if Greyson could deal with Floyd's asshole past – and assholes from his past.

Something told him Greyson would love to see Brett again anyway.

"Okay," Greyson gasped a moment later, pulling back from his new boyfriend with a laugh. "We should get in before we're too wet."

"Among other things," Floyd murmured, a smile spreading across his lips as he led Greyson by the hand to the tattoo shop.

He loved the way Chase's eyes flickered between them as they trotted into the shop together, Greyson going first and pulling Floyd in out of the rain.

"Welcome back," Chase smirked. "I see you had a good lunch."

Floyd knew he was glowing, but he flipped Chase the middle finger. "Shut up."

"Have fun back there," Chase added anyway, leaning on his elbows on the counter and giving them an even broader grin.

Greyson shook his head and followed Floyd into the back room again. The way Greyson watched Floyd as he shrugged off his shirt and the light bandages made Floyd's cheeks flush, but he focused on reloading the ink cartridge.

Maybe for the last time.

"Okay," Floyd laughed as he took a seat on the stool and rolled toward Greyson. "You're gonna have to stop watching me like that."

"Like what?" Greyson was obnoxiously grinning.

"Like *that*," Floyd laughed. "Let me finish my goddamn work unless you want these feathers to be all crooked."

"Will I embarrass you?"

"Oh, I picked an asshole," Floyd groaned, wiping down Greyson's arm with sanitizer.

Greyson snickered. "You know me."

"I do." Floyd glanced up at him. "How about we spend tomorrow together, though...?" He wasn't sure Greyson would want him to stay overnight yet – he did seem to have issues with that – but he could do this, at least.

"How about tonight?"

Floyd met Greyson's eyes. They were as warm as his smile. Greyson leaned up for an impulsive peck on Floyd's lips, then lowered himself back onto the tattoo chair.

Floyd leaned down to return the peck. "God, yes," he murmured. Greyson was finally letting him in, and... well, he didn't have time to get emotional about it. He pulled back again to grab gloves. "Now stop watching me."

Greyson laughed but didn't protest, settling back and closing his eyes as he stretched out his bare arm. His body was totally relaxed under the bright lights, his fingers lightly curled up. It was the ultimate display of trust, and Floyd's whole chest warmed up.

Tonight.

He'd tell Greyson everything tonight, and maybe he'd learn a little more, too. Or maybe it would be gradual. Maybe Greyson would never want to talk about some of the things that plagued him.

That was fine, too.

Floyd would take this man however he wanted to give himself to him, and he'd love him just as much no matter what.

The gun buzzed in his hand, and Floyd brought his keen focus to hone in on the next hundred dots he had to imprint on Greyson's skin.

FLOYD'S LIPS WERE SOFT, HIS HANDS GENTLE AS THEY CUPPED Greyson's cheek and side. Greyson's arms stung, and for the first time in a long time, he didn't crave even more sensation.

He actually didn't like the sting across his inner arms, along the scar tissue, and down to his wrist.

"Don't bump against the wall," Floyd murmured, and Greyson laughed quietly as they moved out of the foyer toward the staircase.

"I can handle a little bump."

"Hey. Not on my fresh art," Floyd clicked his tongue.

Greyson laughed, taking Floyd by the hand to lead him upstairs. He'd bumped his arms a few times when they went to grab supper before heading home, and during the subsequent drink. A cider each, a pizza to share, and God, he loved being around Floyd.

When the bedroom door clicked shut behind him, he let Floyd push him over toward the bed, grinning as he walked backward. Just before he fell, he hooked his fingers through Floyd's belt loops to yank him down with him.

"Ooh!" Floyd laughed, shifting and squirming against him as their torsos rubbed together, legs tangling. They both laughed then, pulling their feet free so that Floyd could straddle him.

Greyson loved having Floyd on top of him, all six-foot-something of him. Especially when he was unbuttoning his shirt and shoving it off, showing off the tattoos along his stomach and sides and shoulders and arms...

He was fucking gorgeous. Greyson wondered why he didn't have tattoos across his chest yet, but he could ask another time.

"Careful," Floyd murmured, tossing his shirt aside and unbuttoning Greyson's to see his chest and torso. "I'll leave your shirt on to keep an extra layer of protection."

"You have to be so fuckin' sweet?" Greyson grumbled.

"I know, right? I should be an asshole and make you lift me off the ground and fuck me."

Greyson winced at the idea of every inch of his arms being wrapped around Floyd's thighs and up his back, supporting his weight. *That* part was hot, but on freshly-tattooed skin? "Ouch. But once my arms heal..."

"Oh, God, yes." Floyd braced himself over Greyson, one tattooed arm on either side of his head as he leaned down to press their lips together again.

It was the easiest thing in the world to fall into bed with Floyd, flirting and teasing the whole damn time like they weren't already about to fuck.

Or maybe make love.

Floyd's touch was tender as he pulled Greyson's jeans and underwear off, scooting down the bed while staying careful not to touch Greyson's arms.

Greyson splayed his arms out so that wouldn't be a problem, grinning as Floyd's gaze wandered up his body from his half-hard cock to his chest, then his face. "You like the results of all my crunches?"

"Do I ever."

Floyd leaned down to press a few light kisses along the skin revealed by his unbuttoned shirt – along the chest, under a nipple, then along his ribs and down his stomach, over his rippling abs, to his hip.

"Mmm," Greyson moaned quietly, and then Floyd's mouth was around his cock, sucking in a few gentle teases before Floyd pulled away. "Oh, you motherfuckin' tease."

Floyd laughed and winked up the length of his body. He pressed one more smooch to the tip. "I'll make up for it."

"You'd better fuck me like nothing else," Greyson idly threatened, spreading his legs further apart and grinning.

Floyd's eyes widened for a moment. "You want that? Oh, God, yes."

"I'm... flexible," Greyson teased, then winked. "In multiple ways."

Floyd was already grabbing for a condom and lube, and Greyson laughed at the urgency he suddenly had.

Greyson couldn't stop watching Floyd's eyes as Floyd cracked open the lube. Then, those sweet eyes rose to lock on his own, watching him with concern and care.

Fingers pushed inside and Greyson breathed out, his stomach tightening. "Hnnh."

"Oh, you're so hot." Greyson couldn't look away from Floyd even as Floyd's fingers pushed further inside, warming and filling and lightly stretching him. More importantly, those fingers stroked along his prostate with a distinctive little jolt of pleasure that turned into a slightly stronger one.

Within a minute, Greyson was moaning and writhing

against the covers, his head rolling back as his back arched off the bed. The fingers pulled out, leaving him disappointingly empty until the condom-clad tip pressed at his opening.

Floyd knelt between his legs as he pushed in, then grabbed Greyson's thighs and hauled them up his lap.

"Yes," Greyson moaned, wrapping his legs around Floyd's waist as the thick warmth pushed slowly inside him, inch by goddamn inch.

Oh, God, that felt incredible. He'd almost forgotten how *good* a hot cock inside him could be!

And then Floyd was setting into motion with quick, skilled thrusts of his hips, filling Greyson deeply each time. Greyson's back arched again and he gasped as the head of that thick cock rubbed against his prostate, making his whole body tense and his cock harden even more.

He pulsed with pleasure already, his muscles twitching.

And when he opened his eyes, Floyd was still watching, his eyes dark with arousal and lips curled up in a beautiful little smile.

Greyson moaned and grabbed Floyd's shoulders, letting his legs slide away from Floyd's waist so he could pull Floyd against him.

Their bodies crashed together in a wave of warmth and passion, nipples brushing nipples as Floyd's hot, heavy weight blanketed Greyson. Greyson arched up against him and kissed him hard, panting his arousal into his mouth.

"You're so fucking hot," Floyd moaned, his voice already strained as he fucked Greyson into the mattress just as hard and fast as Greyson had asked of him.

"Christ, so are you!" Greyson managed. His body

throbbed with pleasure, the rhythm pulling him along in his pleasure. All he could do was fumble between them for his own cock and jerk it off.

Floyd pushed his hand away to take over the job, stroking him at the same quick, hard pace his cock pounded into him...

And yet, they couldn't seem to look away from each other. Something wild and magnetic and absolutely impossible to escape was in their locked gazes, deep in Floyd's eyes.

It was unmistakable, but Greyson didn't dare breathe it out. They'd known each other years ago, and only a few weeks this time around. It was too soon.

The thought was driven from his eyes moments later as his whole body pulsed and shivered. He was so fucking close...

"Fuck, *yes*!" Greyson moaned. He didn't care that his arms stung as he pulled Floyd's back close to him, his arms wrapped around Floyd's waist to keep their weight together like they could meld together.

And then he was spilling over the edge into hot, raw-edged pleasure that tore a cry of arousal from his throat. His body squeezed and pulsed and pleasure spilled from him as he writhed against the pillow. Floyd's lips only pressed against his throat and collarbone to set his nerves even more on edge, making him thrust his hips forward into Floyd's fist.

"F-Floyd! Yes! Hnnh...!"

"Y-Yeah!" Floyd grunted, his cock stuttering to a halt for a moment deep within Greyson before he was fucking him again, the bed surely close to creaking with the force. These thrusts were unconscious, full of pleasure spilling from him and caught by the condom.

But Greyson did get to enjoy the expressions of unashamed, unfiltered pleasure that crossed Floyd's face.

He pressed kisses against Floyd's lips until Floyd's eyes cleared of their orgasmic haze and he could focus on Greyson's face again.

"Hey," Greyson smirked. "You were a long way away just there."

"No," Floyd murmured, his voice deep and sincere as he slowly pulled out and flopped against Greyson to let them recover. "I was right here."

Greyson's heart clenched and he ran his hand slowly up Floyd's back as Floyd held him close. They were gazing into each other's eyes again, neither of them saying a word.

A long minute later, an abrupt smile crossed Floyd's lips and he finally broke the gaze with a little laugh, pulling Greyson in and rolling onto his side.

Greyson let Floyd pull him in against his chest, not complaining for a moment about those arms being wrapped around him. He still ached with pleasure and the faint desire to be fucked again, but he could wait until morning for that.

God, he was tired. It was probably the constant pain and the long day of doing nothing, lying perfectly still in the tattoo chair. He'd cashed in a couple favors to get someone to cover his weekend classes, but even that was worth it.

He'd do anything to be around Floyd.

Greyson tingled with the pleasurable warmth and closeness, his eyes drifting shut. The soft breaths exhaled against the back of his neck were the last thing he felt before sleep.

The smell of eggs hit Greyson's nose at about the same second his stomach rumbled. He stretched and rolled in bed before he forcing himself to get up and dressed.

When Greyson peeked around the kitchen corner, he had to smile. Floyd was singing under his breath as he cooked eggs and pancakes. He actually shimmied on the spot, too, brandishing a fork like a baton.

"Morning."

"Oh!" Floyd jumped, then laughed, putting down the fork. "Good morning. I didn't even hear you. Stealthy."

"You *have* lost all the old skills," Greyson half-smiled. He knew better than to tease Floyd much about it, given his feelings about their past life, but he thought he'd earned a bit of leeway by now.

Floyd clicked his tongue but smiled. "Thank God."

Greyson knew what he meant. Frankly, he was a bit jealous. He'd take a little relaxation over having to sit facing every door and eying every passerby twice. "What's to eat?"

"Eggs and pancakes. You're out of bacon," Floyd chuckled. "You hungry?"

"Starved." Greyson sat at the table, fidgeting with his utensils. "Thanks for breakfast."

"Don't thank me 'til you know if the pancakes are any good. It's kind of hard to screw up eggs, though."

"Long as you don't put milk in them," Greyson nodded.

Floyd looked guiltily up at him.

"*No*," Greyson gasped and laughed. "Oh, man, you don't."

"I always have!"

Greyson laughed richly and shrugged. "Fine. If there's enough ketchup."

Floyd brought that to the table, then their plates of food.

Greyson stopped him by grabbing his collar before he

could pull back and get them drinks. He leaned in and pressed a gentle kiss to Floyd's lips.

Floyd cupped his cheek and kissed him back, his lips tasting faintly minty. Mmm, fresh and tasty. Then, Floyd pulled back and winked. "Juice?"

"Yeah," Greyson agreed without even thinking. He'd have preferred coffee, but Floyd brought over what looked like fresh-pressed apple juice and he forgot about that instantly. The thought of coffee made him remember that he had to get in touch with Darren and Lyle, though. They'd been oddly quiet.

Floyd gathered their dishes after they ate, then waved his hand at Greyson. "Go to the bathroom and grab your tattoo lotion. It's the one that looks like lube but isn't."

Greyson laughed. "What if I grab the lube?" he winked.

"That depends," Floyd smirked. Then his face fell. "But I gotta work today."

Greyson groaned. "Me too. I was trying to forget that." He headed to the bathroom to grab the white bottle, and when he came out, Floyd was sitting on the couch.

"Off with your shirt," Floyd grinned.

"I think I *did* grab the wrong one," Greyson smirked as he flopped next to Floyd and yanked off his shirt. He winced when fabric slid over his skin.

Floyd smoothed the lotion over his fingers, then spread it across Greyson's skin starting at his shoulders.

Oh, the cooling lotion slicked into his stinging skin felt like heaven. Greyson resisted a moan of pleasure but breathed out a pleased little sigh.

"Good, huh?" Floyd chuckled quietly. "That feeling never quite gets old. You're already healing well. The flaking will start soon, though."

"I can handle that," Greyson assured him. "I'm used to it now."

"Oooh." Floyd took one of Greyson's arms into his lap to smooth the lotion across his forearm, effortlessly running his palm over the inside and outsides to rub lotion down to his wrist. "Look who's an expert now."

Greyson laughed quietly, gazing up at Floyd as he worked. The tender care with which his hands moved made him smile. "My parents are coming around, you know."

"Yeah?" Floyd murmured, pausing for a moment before he rubbed back up to Greyson's bicep and up to his shoulder, then patted him to get him to give him his other arm.

"Mmhmm." Greyson didn't want to brag, but it was true. "And yours...?"

Floyd winced.

"Sorry." *Is this too fast?*

"No, it's – it's okay." Floyd cleared his throat. "Um, I don't know if I can... be around them right now."

Greyson sharply looked from Floyd's hand up to his face, but Floyd was watching his own hands work across Greyson's inner arm. "Oh."

Floyd was quiet until he worked the lotion in all the way up to Greyson's arm. There was a lot he wasn't saying right now. Greyson knew exactly what that expression looked like, and what it felt like inside him, too.

Pain or not, Greyson slipped his arms around Floyd's waist and pulled him in for a silent hug. Floyd resisted for a moment before his body relaxed gradually.

"I have something I should tell you, too," Floyd murmured once Greyson let go of him. "Uh, about Brett."

Floyd's ex? I keep thinking I won't hear his name again, and then I do. Greyson sucked in a slow breath, then nodded. "What about him?"

"I want to be upfront with you so you don't think I'm playing games. He's going to be at the reunion, and I think he's trying to... I don't know, pressure me into going with him?" Floyd furrowed his brows as he looked at Greyson. "I don't really get it."

Greyson's eyes narrowed. "Is he harassing you?"

"Only on Grindr. I deleted it. Got sick of it, and..." Then, Floyd turned red as he glanced away. "Yeah."

"And what?" Greyson asked, his lips quirking up.

"And I don't think I need it anymore." Floyd gazed at him, the question in his eyes.

His heart thumping, Greyson nodded. "Er, getting back to Brett – are you in danger?"

Floyd's chuckle broke the tension a little. "No, no," Floyd assured him quickly. "I just wanted to warn you he'll be lurking around like a... fly on the wall, most likely."

"Okay." Greyson bristled with protective instincts still – which answered Floyd's unspoken question. But there was something else here, and it took Greyson a moment to see him. By telling him about Brett being around, Floyd trusted him not to go beat the shit out of him again.

Ugh. He had to live up to that better person he was trying to be. He licked his lips. "Okay. You can handle this, then, but... tell me if you need anything. Seeing us together at the reunion will probably scare him off. Is he still even living here?"

"No. He's back in town for the reunion and probably visiting family or something. For, like, the last couple weeks. It's weird. Maybe he's bumming around," Floyd scowled.

Greyson breathed out a quiet sigh. "Yeah." He tapped his toe on the ground now, still leaning into Floyd.

"What?"

"I should probably talk about my stuff, too." *It's been weeks of trying not to. I don't know how to even approach it.*

Floyd nodded slowly, squeezing Greyson around the shoulders gently. "Only if you want to."

"I used to hurt myself because I get... really wound up. It's like all the anxiety or guilt or whatever gets under my skin and it's the only way I could think of to let it out," Greyson said. He spoke quickly, not giving himself the chance to realize what he was admitting and shut down. "I still *want* to sometimes, but I haven't in a long time. Well, I still pinch myself sometimes to snap out of the moment, or... the tattoos... um, they hit that same button."

"Is that a bad thing?" Floyd asked. His expression was neutral but invested in what Greyson was saying.

Greyson slowly shook his head. "It's just training my brain not to go for the first option. *Just,* I say, like it's easy."

Floyd chuckled and pressed his lips to Greyson's shoulder. "I'm proud of you, though. We both went through stuff. I turned it outward, you turned it inward."

When Floyd put it that way, it made sense. Greyson nodded. "Suppose so."

"I'll never push you to talk about anything specific," Floyd said quietly. "But I forgive you for everything that happened with Brett. And I think the world of you. It says a lot that you chose to quit rather than be on the wrong side of justice back there in Alberta."

Greyson's heart squeezed as he shifted to rest his head on Floyd's shoulder. He closed his eyes for a few moments, then murmured, "Thanks." For the first time, the words really sank in: Floyd was *proud* of him.

"And when you do wanna hurt yourself, if you can let me know, I'll try to distract you. Or I'll leave you alone. Whatever you need from me. But I want to see you as much as I can," Floyd chuckled.

"Me too," Greyson laughed. "I love..." he trailed off, then cleared his throat and glanced quickly at Floyd. *Is that gonna freak him out?*

"I love you," Floyd murmured quietly. Then Floyd's warm lips met his in a long, warm kiss, as Greyson's chest flooded with relief.

When they pulled back, Greyson was breathless and smiling back. "I love you too."

"I also love making sure my employees open the shop on time, and I'm sure you love getting to your classes on time..." Floyd trailed off with a mischievous grin.

"Oh, shit." Greyson checked his watch. "Ohhh, that's a horrible cliffhanger."

Floyd laughed. "Can we hang out today after work, though? We were talking about it last night and then it became all about... well, last night."

Greyson smirked. "Yeah." He pecked Floyd's lips a few more times, then rose to his feet with a reluctant groan. "You'd better get going."

"Chase will have a field day if I come in wearing yesterday's clothes," Floyd chuckled.

Greyson laughed as he walked Floyd to the door, kissing him a few more times along the way.

Then Floyd pulled back with a frustrated groan. "I *gotta* go."

"Mmhmm." Greyson pecked Floyd's lips.

"You devil." Floyd swatted Greyson's ass with a grin, then pulled open the door to escape while Greyson laughed.

Only after he was gone did Greyson think about Brett again. Meeting him seemed like a tiny obstacle in comparison to their bond. With Greyson by his side, Floyd could handle this on his own. Greyson wasn't going to let Floyd walk into that reunion alone.

CHAPTER
Thirty~One
FLOYD

"Oof, no. My arm's too sore. If you didn't make me do *so* many chest presses..." Floyd complained with a playful wink.

Greyson snorted. "Oh, blame me for you actually working those biceps." He squeezed Floyd's arm, pressing the car door lock button on his remote. "You sure about this?"

Floyd drew a breath and let it out, then nodded sharply. "Positive." Floyd linked arms with Greyson.

His boldness had grown leaps and bounds in the last couple weeks. So had Greyson's, in subtle ways, as his tattoos healed beautifully. Although Greyson didn't want him to get burned for this, Floyd really wanted to test it out. A reunion was the perfect place to announce who he was – and whom he was with.

They walked toward their old high school building, nudging each other as they pointed out the tiny, familiar details: its yellowish brown bricks, the rows of windows up to their old classrooms, and the hugeness of the parking lot that, in winter, hosted piles of snow from the plows.

"It's weird being here again... especially this time of year,"

Greyson laughed as they stepped through the open front doors. The doors were decorated with streamers and balloons to welcome them.

Almost the moment they stepped into the school doors, they spotted a woman sitting behind a registration table. She greeted them cheerily, her smile freezing for a moment when she spotted their linked arms.

"Floyd...?"

Floyd couldn't say he recognized her, but he nodded. Of course everyone would know him. "Floyd Turner. This is Greyson Peters."

"Ah, yes, I see you both. Welcome!" She could hardly keep her eye off their linked arms. "Here, take your name tags..."

Finally, Floyd spotted her name tag: Libby. "Oh, you were – I think we had math together."

"We did! Hello again."

"Hi. How's... life going?" Floyd smiled.

"Great! I'm working out in Moncton now, but I came back to town for the reunion. You run a tattoo shop, don't you? I've heard about it."

"Right, I do," Floyd nodded. He unlinked arms with Greyson long enough to stick his tag onto his shirt, leaning over for a peek at the guest list. "How many people are here?"

"Oh, lots. Just about everyone who RSVP'd already!"

Floyd eyed Greyson. If he hadn't driven so slowly...

"Not my fault we got stuck behind the delivery truck," Greyson laughed.

Libby laughed and pointed them through to the gym. It was decorated with more streamers and balloons, but it was still the same old gym.

Floyd smiled as he glanced around, then looked at Greyson. "*This* place."

"It wasn't so bad," Greyson shrugged.

Floyd snorted. *Maybe not for you.* The locker room had been his least favorite spot of the whole school. He just glanced toward it and scoffed.

It took Greyson a moment, but then he nodded slightly. "Ah. Come on, let's get punch." He put his hand on Floyd's back to steer him over to the punch.

"Hey, man. Sweet tats!"

It was Ashton, the little asshole. *Bet he's not a star soccer player.* He wasn't ripped like one, anyway. Floyd smiled back and reached out for a quick handshake. "Thanks. Long time no see. How are you doing?"

"Oh, not bad. I'm working in tech now."

"Oh?" Floyd seemed to remember him making fun of geeks in his day. "Came around to technology?"

"Got offered a job I couldn't resist," Ashton shrugged. He came off a little humbler than before, but still pretty full of himself. "The punch is great. There's an open bar over there, too. Only beer and cider."

Greyson nodded. "Great. Just what we need."

The music was playing quietly for now, tables and chairs around the gym and a dancing floor cleared off for later that night.

"Let's go get cider," Floyd suggested and steered Greyson over there with an arm around his shoulders. He leaned in to murmur, "You still cool with this?"

"Very."

Floyd smiled at the way Greyson put it, then stole a quick kiss before buying cider. The proceeds were going to this year's graduating class charity project, apparently.

And then, just as they had their cider bottles open, there he was: Brett.

Brett looked like he hadn't aged a day. He still had that mop of ugly brown hair, but he was pretty. His eyes had attracted Floyd before.

Floyd still remembered the sight of them black and blue as he spat blood out of his mouth and rebounded on Floyd to get his goddamn work partner out of his life before he took care of him.

Floyd's arm around Greyson's shoulders tightened, but he didn't flinch at Brett – just smiled. "Hello. You haven't changed a bit."

Brett looked taken aback. "Floyd?" He was staring down at Floyd's tattooed arms, then at Greyson. "Oh, Greyson."

Greyson nodded once, but he didn't make a move.

Floyd interrupted the intense eye contact going on between the two by clearing his throat. "This is my boyfriend. I'm sure you remember him, Brett."

Brett looked almost sick. He glowered for a moment before he folded his arms, swigging from his bottle. "Ah, yeah. I've seen him around."

Somehow, looking at that obnoxious face was so much more bearable than Floyd had feared. He felt utterly safe with Greyson's arm around his waist.

"How have you been?" Greyson asked, his voice even and cheery, too. Floyd almost grinned: he was playing along perfectly.

Brett cleared his throat, then dug his phone out of his pocket. "Oh, you know. Busy with work. I might have to leave for that soon."

Floyd tried not to laugh at how obviously fake that was. "Right. Good seeing you anyway." He spotted a few more interesting people – friends from his last couple years of high school. He turned from Brett to head to them, and

Greyson stayed with him to head over and greet them instead.

It took about twenty minutes before he felt the adrenaline completely settle again, but the whole time, he felt so open and... well, strong.

Being able to look Brett in the eye and laugh at him was a freedom Floyd had never dreamed of, and it meant so much that Greyson was right there with him. He hoped it helped Greyson feel better about his role in their breakup, too.

And then, the reunion turned to everything Floyd had expected: former classmates comparing careers, babies, and cars. Some were obviously trying to pick someone up, and others had brought plus-ones. All of them were shocked at first to see how close Floyd stood to Greyson, but they hid their reactions to varying degrees. When Floyd bragged that they'd been together for a couple weeks, they got plenty of congratulations – more than a few of those well wishes said in a certain jealous tone.

A few beers and hours later, the dancing started, and Greyson pulled Floyd to the floor for an hour or so of it. They danced with old buddies sometimes, letting loose and reminiscing, and sometimes just by themselves.

Best of all, Floyd didn't even see Brett once more. He could put up with obnoxious old classmates calling them the wrong names or trying to subtly brag about their own careers.

Just before midnight, though, when he'd waited off the last of his ciders, Greyson took Floyd's hand and pulled him close. He leaned in, his lips breathing warm air across Floyd's ear. It made him shudder with pleasure. "Before one more person comes over to show off their receding hairline and baby photos..."

Floyd burst out laughing and squeezed Greyson's hand. "Let's get out of here," he agreed.

As they walked out through the warm evening, swinging each other's hands the whole way, Floyd could hardly stop smiling.

"You trusted me back there," Greyson said quietly as they reached the car.

Floyd paused, squeezing Greyson's hand once more before letting go. "I did. I do."

Greyson cupped his cheeks. They were in the middle of the parking lot, but he didn't rush through the kiss, leaning in slowly to kiss Floyd.

By the time Greyson was done, Floyd laughed breathlessly, running his hand back through Greyson's hair. "Let's definitely head home."

"Home," Greyson promised with a broad smile.

FLOYD

"MAN, YOU WERE HOLDING OUT ON ME!"

Floyd laughed as he leaned back into the couch, avoiding Kevin's punches to his shoulder. "We didn't officially get together until... a couple weeks ago. And I wanted to surprise you."

"Well, you did!" Kevin grinned. He was home for a week before he flew out for his next training session. Floyd had brought Greyson to Cam's house to see Kevin while he was visiting the brothers.

"A little birdie told me that you were together," Jackson clicked his tongue from the background. "But you've been all sneaky."

"I just wanted to enjoy the first few weeks..."

"...and take off early from work all the time," Chase smirked. "Like that's not obvious."

Floyd's cheeks flushed.

Greyson laughed as he shook Kevin's hand. "I've heard a lot about you."

"Oh no," Kevin groaned, shoving Floyd. "It's not true."

Floyd smirked. "Too late. I told him everything except where the tattoo is."

This prompted a wave of laughter from the rest of the guys as they handed over beers. Floyd took his with a wry little smile. He'd never drunk so much since hanging out with them, but he felt confident they wouldn't let him go too far.

"Hey, you two, now that you're being out about it, come to brunch tomorrow," Chase added, waving his bottle at them both. "And barbecues again! Jesus, we haven't seen either of you for like a month."

Greyson relaxed and smiled as he was invited back. "Thanks. We will."

"Free food? Fuck, yeah," Floyd smirked. "Uh, we were just... you know, we didn't want to intrude."

All three brothers stared at him with raised eyebrows. "On?" Cam asked.

"Brother time?" Floyd offered. It sounded ridiculous even saying it.

"Oh, you idiot," Kevin laughed, punching his arm again as he headed to the couch and scooted over to make room for them both. "Remember when I said you'd be welcome anytime? Just like me, or Ryan, or the other guys."

Floyd's cheeks flushed as he settled a bowl of chips in his lap. "That, and... you know, we've been busy."

"Ooooh." There was a mix of groans and laughter, and Floyd laughed, rolling his head back. *Shoot me now. They'll never let us live it down.*

Jackson leaned over and caught Floyd's eyes. "Problem with being part of this family is you're now fair game."

"What?"

Jackson grabbed the chip bowl. Floyd had to grab it right

back to get another handful before he let it go. Floyd laughed anyway. It was a crazy family he'd been welcomed into, but hearing the word made him glow.

As he caught Greyson's eyes, he could tell his boyfriend was thinking the same thing as he looked with curious fondness around at his new friends. Greyson's family was better than Floyd's, but only time would tell if they would learn to be the family he needed.

Somehow, Floyd had thought the Riley family was welcoming Chase in just because he was Jackson's boyfriend, but... they weren't *that* tight-knit. After all, their mutual buddy Ryan still came out for beers, and they'd welcomed Greyson over for a barbecue within hours of knowing him.

And now he had a second family about as officially as possible. Whether Kevin had told him what Floyd had said about his family, or Chase had hinted to them, they'd welcomed him in. As he watched everyone handing around beers, fighting over the TV remote, and sharing food, Floyd's cheeks hurt from smiling.

Family was made, not born.

Slam (The Riley Brothers #5)

"I DON'T WANT TO BE THE POSTER BOY."

Kevin Shaw isn't about to come out. He's only got a year to prove himself in the major leagues of hockey. He has to train hard, get his big break, and ignore everything he wants to do in the showers to his new teammate, Matty.

Matty O'Brien is secretly terrified he won't hack it after being called up to the team. He's perpetually single and feeling the ache of always being the wingman and never the boyfriend. But the way Kevin watches him makes him feel like a star for the first time.

One spontaneous kiss sends them both scurrying for shelter. Locker room gossip could be enough to end their careers. In a choice between their passions for the game and each other, there's no winning… unless they find a way to have both.

Slam is the fifth book in The Riley Brothers, a low-angst series filled with brotherly banter and small-town smiles. This steamy, standalone gay romance novel can be enjoyed on its own, and promises a happily-ever-after ending.

Grind

Brooklyn Boys:

Electric Sunshine

Live Wire

Boiling Point

F-Word:

Flaunt

Freak

Faux

Forever

Freedom

After:

Afterburn

Afterglow

Aftermath

Shared Universes:

Shelter

Adore

Miracle

Redemption

Limelight

Barely Regal